THE GRAPHIC NOVEL

Mary Shelley

Frankenstein: The Graphic Novel
Quick Text Version

Mary Shelley

First US Edition

Published by: Classical Comics Ltd

Acknowledgments: Every effort has been made to trace copyright holders of
material reproduced in this book. Any rights not acknowledged here will be
acknowledged in subsequent editions if notice is given to Classical Comics Ltd.

All enquiries should be addressed to:
Classical Comics Ltd.
PO Box 7280
Litchborough
Towcester
NN12 9AR
United Kingdom
Tel: 0845 812 3000

info@classicalcomics.com
www.classicalcomics.com

ISBN: 978-1-906332-50-1

Printed in China by SURE Print & Design
using biodegradable vegetable inks on environmentally friendly paper.
This material can be disposed of by recycling,
incineration for energy recovery, composting and biodegradation.

Jason Cardy and Kat Nicholson would like to thank Kate Derrick and
Dylan Cook for their help with preparing the pages for coloring.
The publishers would like to acknowledge the design assistance of
Greg Powell in the completion of this book.

Contents

Dramatis Personæ

Victor Frankenstein

Frankenstein's Monster

Elizabeth Lavenza
Victor's adopted sister

Robert Walton
Adventurer

The Ship's Master

The Ship's Lieutenant

Alphonse Frankenstein
Victor's father

Caroline Frankenstein
Victor's mother

Ernest Frankenstein
Victor's brother

William Frankenstein
Victor's brother

Henry Clerval
Victor's friend

Justine Moritz
Servant to Frankenstein's household

Dramatis Personæ

Monsieur Krempe
Professor of Natural Philosophy, University of Ingolstadt

Monsieur Waldman
Professor of Chemistry, University of Ingolstadt

Lawyer
States the charge against Justine Moritz

Old Woman
Gives evidence against Justine Mortiz

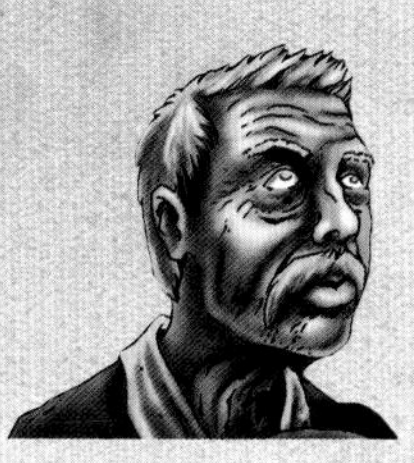

Monsieur DeLacy
Cottage dweller

Agatha DeLacy
Daughter of Monsieur DeLacy

Felix DeLacy
Son of Monsieur DeLacy

Turkish Merchant

Safie
Daughter of the Turkish Merchant

Mr. Kirwin
Magistrate

Fisherman

Genevan Judge

Prologue

Mary Shelley's literary masterpiece ***Frankenstein*** was unleashed upon the world in 1818. It was written before the days of steam travel, when the world seemed a much larger place than it does today. Far-off places were out of the reach of all but the bravest adventurers; and in those unknown places it was possible that things could exist – even things created by human beings – that would terrify anyone who saw them.

Science was progressing at an astounding pace. It seemed that anything and everything was possible, as the human race found new and more powerful ways to create and also to destroy.

At the same time, medical science was finding new ways to heal the sick and to revive the dying; and it started to raise questions about the nature of life itself. If the dying can be revived, then could the dead also be brought back to life? How about a dead person that had been assembled from the parts of other dead people? Could that be given life too?

Where would it all end? Would this all go too far? And if so, what would the consequences be?

Indeed, in this early world of advancing medical science, anything and everything seemed possible...

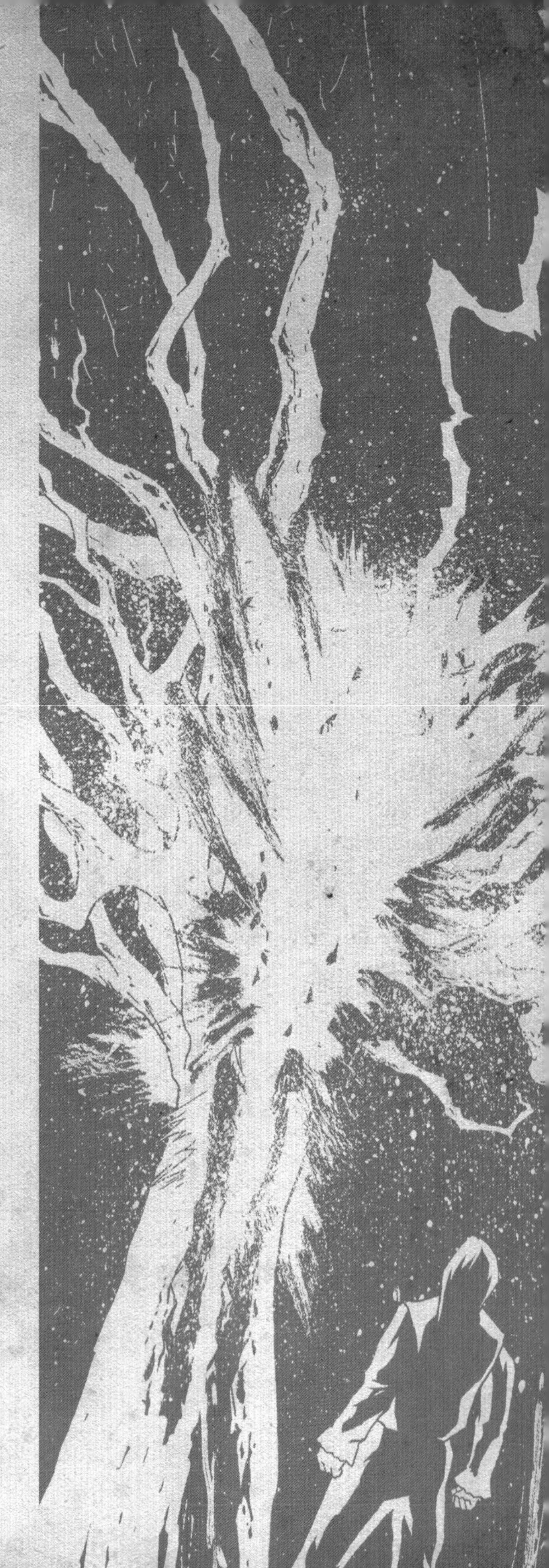

FROM THE LETTERS OF ROBERT WALTON:
LETTER I - DECEMBER 11TH
MY DEAR SISTER...
I AM ALREADY FAR NORTH OF LONDON.
THE NORTH POLE IS A LAND FULL OF WONDERS AND BEAUTY, WHERE THE SUN NEVER SETS.

FOR AS LONG AS I CAN REMEMBER, THIS JOURNEY HAS BEEN MY DREAM.

I DESERVE TO DO SOMETHING GREAT!
LETTER II - MARCH 28TH
TIME PASSES SO SLOWLY HERE, MARGARET, AND I AM LONELY.

LETTER III - JULY 7TH
WE ARE FAR, FAR NORTH NOW, BUT I WILL BE CAREFUL.

LETTER IV - AUGUST 5TH
LAST MONDAY, OUR SHIP WAS SURROUNDED BY ICE AND FOG.
WHEN THE FOG FINALLY CLEARED, WE SAW A STRANGE SIGHT.
IT WAS A HUGE MAN, FAR AWAY FROM US. WE WERE STUCK IN THE ICE, SO WE COULDN'T FOLLOW HIM.

IN THE MORNING, THE SAILORS WERE TALKING TO SOMEONE OVERBOARD - IT WAS A MAN STRANDED IN THE ICY COLD.
OUR CAPTAIN WILL LOOK AFTER YOU.
PLEASE TELL ME WHERE YOUR SHIP IS HEADED.
THE NORTH POLE.
HE AGREED TO COME ON BOARD.

I NEVER SAW A MAN IN SUCH A DREADFUL STATE. SLOWLY, WE HELPED HIM TO RECOVER. IT WAS TWO DAYS BEFORE HE COULD SPEAK.

WHAT WERE YOU DOING OUT THERE?
I WAS TRYING TO FIND SOMEONE.
WE SAW HIM -
ON A SLEDGE, ON THE ICE.
DO YOU THINK THE ICE BREAKING DESTROYED HIS SLEDGE?
THE ICE BROKE MUCH LATER -
HE MIGHT HAVE MADE IT TO SAFETY BEFORE THEN.
I'M SURE THAT YOU HAVE MANY QUESTIONS FOR ME.
YOU RESCUED ME, AND HAVE BROUGHT ME BACK TO LIFE!
THE STRANGER SEEMED SUDDENLY DIFFERENT.
AUGUST 13TH
MY NEW FRIEND IS NOW MUCH RECOVERED FROM HIS ILLNESS.

AUGUST 19TH
YESTERDAY HE SAID TO ME...
CAPTAIN WALTON, I HAVE SUFFERED GREATLY. YOU SEEK KNOWLEDGE AS I ONCE DID. YOU MAY LEARN A LOT FROM MY OWN TALE.
MY DESTINY IS SEALED - LISTEN TO MY HISTORY...
VOLUME I
CHAPTER I
MY NAME IS VICTOR FRANKENSTEIN; MY PARENTS WERE FROM GENEVA, WHERE THEY WERE WELL RESPECTED.
MY PARENTS TRAVELED AROUND, AND I WAS BORN WHILE THEY WERE IN NAPLES.

FOR SEVERAL YEARS, I WAS THEIR ONLY CHILD. THEY TRULY LOVED ME.
WHEN I WAS FIVE YEARS OLD, MY MOTHER ADOPTED THE ORPHANED DAUGHTER OF A NOBLEMAN.
ELIZABETH LAVENZA BECAME MORE THAN JUST A SISTER TO ME - FOR I TRULY ADORED HER.
VOLUME I
CHAPTER II
THERE WAS LESS THAN A YEAR BETWEEN US.
MY PARENTS SETTLED IN GENEVA WHEN THEIR SECOND SON WAS BORN...
...THERE, I BECAME GREAT FRIENDS WITH HENRY CLERVAL. HE LOVED TO READ AND WRITE, AS WELL AS ACT.

ELIZABETH WAS LOVELY AND BROUGHT OUT THE BEST IN ALL OF US.
I STUDIED THE WORKS OF GREAT THINKERS.
CORNELIUS
HERE WERE MEN WHO HAD DISCOVERED THE SECRETS OF NATURE.
AND WHAT GLORY WOULD BE MINE, IF I COULD RID MAN OF ILLNESS!
ALBERTUS
WHEN I WAS FIFTEEN, WE SAW A TERRIBLE THUNDERSTORM.

THE THUNDER BURST FROM THE HEAVENS.
KARAKKK!
I WATCHED AS LIGHTNING STRUCK AN OLD OAK TREE.
THE TREE WAS BURNED DOWN TO A STUMP.

THE NEXT MORNING, WE FOUND THE TREE SHATTERED INTO THIN RIBBONS OF WOOD. AT ONCE I BEGAN TO STUDY THE MATHEMATICS AND SCIENCE OF ELECTRICITY.
BUT DESTINY HAD ALREADY DECIDED ON MY DESTRUCTION.
VOLUME I
CHAPTER III
WHEN I WAS SEVENTEEN, I WAS DUE TO LEAVE FOR INGOLSTADT UNIVERSITY...
...BUT ELIZABETH CAUGHT SCARLET FEVER. SHE RECOVERED, BUT MY MOTHER BECAME SICK FROM TENDING TO HER.

My children, your marriage together would make me very happy.
Elizabeth, you must be a mother to my younger children.
I hope to see you in another world...

SHE DIED CALMLY.

MY MOTHER WAS DEAD...
...BUT WE STILL HAD DUTIES TO PERFORM. ELIZABETH LOOKED AFTER US AND GAVE COMFORT.

FINALLY, THE DAY CAME FOR ME TO LEAVE FOR INGOLSTADT.
WRITE OFTEN, VICTOR.
I LOVED MY FAMILY, ELIZABETH, AND CLERVAL; BUT I LONGED TO ACQUIRE KNOWLEDGE.

AFTER A LONG JOURNEY, I ARRIVED AT INGOLSTADT.
NEXT MORNING, I DELIVERED MY LETTERS OF INTRODUCTION.

THE FIRST WENT TO MONSIEUR KREMPE - A PROFESSOR OF PHILOSOPHY WHOM I RESPECTED, YET INSTANTLY DISLIKED.
YOU HAVE SPENT YOUR TIME STUDYING THIS NONSENSE?
YES.
WHAT A WASTE OF YOUR TIME!
YOU MUST BEGIN AGAIN WITH NEW STUDIES!
I WENT INTO THE LECTURE THEATER AND SAW A VERY DIFFERENT PROFESSOR - MONSIEUR WALDMAN.
ANCIENT TEACHERS OF SCIENCE PROMISED MUCH, BUT PRODUCED NOTHING.
THE MODERN MASTERS PROMISE LITTLE, YET REVEAL MUCH TO US ABOUT NATURE AND LIFE ITSELF.
THEY HAVE ACQUIRED NEW POWERS OVER HEAVEN AND EARTH.
SOON I HAD ONLY ONE THOUGHT: TO EXPLORE UNKNOWN POWERS AND REVEAL THE DEEPEST MYSTERIES OF CREATION.

VOLUME I
CHAPTER IV
MONSIEUR WALDMAN AND I BECAME FRIENDS.
TWO YEARS PASSED, AND WITH HIS HELP, I MADE DISCOVERIES THAT BUILT MY REPUTATION AT THE UNIVERSITY.
I WAS INTERESTED IN ANYTHING THAT LIVED. MOST OF ALL, I WANTED TO KNOW HOW LIFE WAS CREATED.
TO UNDERSTAND LIFE, WE MUST FIRST UNDERSTAND DEATH.
TO ME, A CHURCHYARD WAS JUST A PLACE FULL OF DEAD BODIES THAT HAD BECOME FOOD FOR WORMS.
I SPENT DAYS AND NIGHTS EXAMINING DEAD BODIES. I SAW HOW THEY DECAYED, AND I EXAMINED EVERY LITTLE DETAIL...
...UNTIL, AFTER WEEKS OF WORK, I DISCOVERED...
...THE SECRET OF LIFE!

I KNEW HOW TO GIVE LIFE TO LIFELESS MATTER.
YET TO PREPARE THE BODY FOR ANIMATION WITH FIBERS, MUSCLES AND VEINS SEEMED IMPOSSIBLE.
I DECIDED TO MAKE THE BODY LARGER SO THAT IT WAS EASIER TO PUT TOGETHER.
IN A SOLITARY ROOM I WORKED ON MY CREATION.

SO DETERMINED WAS I, THAT I MADE MYSELF ILL. I DIDN'T STOP WORKING, EVEN TO LOOK AFTER MYSELF.

VOLUME I
CHAPTER V
ON A DREARY NIGHT IN NOVEMBER, I FINALLY FINISHED.

HE WAS PERFECT.
GREAT GOD!
THE CREATURE OPENED ITS DULL YELLOW EYE.
IT BREATHED AND STARTED TO MOVE!
CHIIIINK!
CLANK!!
BUT THE BEAUTY OF THE DREAM VANISHED, AND MY HEART WAS FILLED WITH HORROR.
CREEEAAKK!!

CLAANK!!
CHIINK!!!
AAARRRRRGGGHHHHH!!

CHINKK!
SMASH!
I COULDN'T BEAR TO SEE HIM.
I RAN OUT OF THE ROOM.
CRASH!
I THREW MYSELF ONTO MY BED TO TRY TO REST - BUT I COULDN'T GET THE MONSTER OUT OF MY MIND...
...AND MY SLEEP WAS BROKEN BY TERRIBLE DREAMS.

I DREAMT OF ELIZABETH, WALKING IN INGOLSTADT.
I EMBRACED HER...
...BUT AS WE KISSED...
...SHE TURNED THE COLOR OF DEATH...

...AND BECAME MY DEAD MOTHER!
AAAAH!
I AWOKE IN HORROR.
SMAAASHHH!!

THERE WAS THE MONSTER I HAD CREATED.
UNGHH... MUH...
I ESCAPED INTO THE COURTYARD...
...WHERE I STAYED ALL NIGHT, LISTENING FOR ANY SOUND OF THE MONSTER.
MY DREAM HAD BECOME MY HELL.

WHEN MORNING CAME, I WALKED THE STREETS OF INGOLSTADT, FEARING THE MONSTER EVERYWHERE I WENT.
I WAS TOO SCARED TO RETURN TO MY APARTMENT.
I DIDN'T REALLY KNOW WHERE I WAS OR WHAT I WAS DOING.
MY HEART POUNDED WITH FEAR.
MY DEAR FRANKENSTEIN!
I'M SO GLAD TO SEE YOU!

I TOOK HIS HAND AND QUICKLY FORGOT MY HORROR.
HENRY CLERVAL!
MY FATHER HAS FINALLY AGREED FOR ME TO ATTEND UNIVERSITY.
I'M SO HAPPY TO SEE YOU. HOW ARE MY FAMILY AND ELIZABETH?
VERY WELL - BUT THEY WOULD REALLY LIKE TO HEAR FROM YOU.
YOU LOOK SO THIN AND PALE.
I HAVEN'T HAD MUCH SLEEP.
I'VE BEEN WORKING HARD ON SOMETHING --
-- SOMETHING THAT I HOPE HAS NOW COME TO AN END.

I TREMBLED AS WE WALKED TO MY COLLEGE.
I WAS AFRAID TO MEET WITH THE CREATURE IN MY APARTMENT...
...BUT EVEN MORE SCARED THAT HENRY SHOULD SEE HIM.
PLEASE WAIT HERE.
I CHECKED THAT MY ENEMY WASN'T THERE.
I CLAPPED MY HANDS WITH JOY AND RAN DOWN FOR HENRY.

I WAS TOO EXCITED TO EAT.
HA-HA HA HA-HAH!!!
HA-HARRH!
VICTOR!
WHAT ON EARTH IS THE MATTER?
HA HAHA HA HA!
WHAT'S CAUSING YOU TO BE LIKE THIS?

I THOUGHT I SAW THE MONSTER IN MY ROOM...
DON'T ASK...
...HE CAN TELL YOU!

SAVE ME!!!
SAVE ME!
I FELL DOWN IN A FIT...
...AND DIDN'T RECOVER FOR A LONG TIME.

HENRY LOOKED AFTER ME FOR SEVERAL MONTHS. HE DIDN'T TELL MY FAMILY OF MY ILLNESS.
SLOWLY, STEADILY, I RECOVERED... ...AND SPRING ARRIVED.
DEAREST HENRY, YOU HAVE LOOKED AFTER ME ALL WINTER, WHEN YOU SHOULD HAVE BEEN STUDYING.
HOW CAN I EVER REPAY YOU?
YOU CAN REPAY ME BY GETTING BETTER -
AND SINCE YOU SEEM WELL ENOUGH TO WRITE, YOUR FATHER AND ELIZABETH WOULD DEARLY LOVE TO RECEIVE A LETTER FROM YOU.
MY FIRST THOUGHTS WERE OF THEM.
THEN THIS LETTER WILL MAKE YOU HAPPY.
IT IS FROM YOUR COUSIN, I BELIEVE.

VOLUME I
CHAPTER VI

DEAR VICTOR,

YOU HAVE BEEN **VERY ILL**, AND DESPITE **HENRY'S LETTERS**, I'VE BEEN SO **WORRIED.**

GET **WELL** AND COME **HOME** - YOUR **FATHER** WOULD BE **SO HAPPY** TO **SEE** YOU.

YOU MAY REMEMBER, SHE WAS A GREAT FAVORITE OF YOURS.
ONE BY ONE, HER BROTHERS AND SISTER DIED, AND JUSTINE WAS CALLED BACK HOME. HER MOTHER WOULD SOMETIMES BEG FOR JUSTINE'S FORGIVENESS, AND THEN BLAME HER FOR CAUSING THE DEATHS OF HER BROTHERS AND SISTER.
BUT JUSTINE'S MOTHER IS AT PEACE NOW; SHE DIED AT THE START OF WINTER.
JUSTINE HAS RETURNED TO US, AND I LOVE HER DEARLY.
I FEEL BETTER FOR WRITING THIS LETTER TO YOU. TAKE CARE OF YOURSELF, AND PLEASE WRITE!
ELIZABETH
DEAR ELIZABETH! I WILL WRITE IMMEDIATELY!
I BEGAN TO RECOVER. TWO WEEKS LATER, I WAS WELL ENOUGH TO LEAVE MY ROOM.

I COULD NEVER TELL HENRY ABOUT WHAT I'D DONE, OR WHAT HAPPENED ON THAT TERRIBLE NIGHT.

CLERVAL CAME TO THE UNIVERSITY TO STUDY ORIENTAL LANGUAGES, AND I STUDIED WITH HIM.
SANSKRIT
I FOUND PEACE IN THE WORKS OF THE ORIENTALISTS.
LIFE SEEMS LIKE SUNSHINE AND ROSES WHEN YOU READ THEIR WRITINGS!
ARABIC

SUMMER PASSED, AND WITH THE ARRIVAL OF WINTER AND SNOW, MY RETURN TO GENEVA WAS DELAYED UNTIL THE FOLLOWING SPRING.
CLERVAL SUGGESTED WE TAKE A FAREWELL TOUR OF INGOLSTADT.
WHAT A TRUE FRIEND!
BLAC
OVER THOSE TWO WEEKS, HE TAUGHT ME TO LOVE NATURE AGAIN, AND TO ENJOY THE CHEERFUL FACES OF CHILDREN.
FOR THE FIRST TIME IN YEARS, I BECAME HAPPY AGAIN.

VOLUME I
CHAPTER VII
I RETURNED TO FIND A LETTER FROM MY FATHER:
DEAR VICTOR,
YOU ARE PROBABLY KEEN TO COME HOME TO US, SO HOW CAN I TELL YOU THIS?
WILLIAM, OUR SWEET, GENTLE CHILD, HAS BEEN MURDERED!
LAST THURSDAY, WE ALL WENT FOR A WALK IN PLAINPALAIS...
NGERIE

ERNEST!
WILLIAM!
IT WAS ALREADY DUSK WHEN WE REALIZED THAT WILLIAM AND ERNEST WERE MISSING.
HAVE YOU SEEN WILLIAM?
WE WERE PLAYING HIDE AND SEEK.
I COULDN'T FIND WILLIAM, AND HE HAS NOT COME BACK!
WE SEARCHED INTO THE NIGHT.
I COULDN'T REST WITH MY BOY OUT THERE ALONE.

AT ABOUT FIVE IN THE MORNING, I FOUND WILLIAM - DEAD.
THE MURDERER'S FINGER MARKS WERE ON HIS NECK.
OH GOD! I'VE KILLED HIM!
I LET WILLIAM WEAR A VALUABLE PICTURE LOCKET OF HIS MOTHER. HE NO LONGER HAS IT - I'M SURE IT'S THE REASON HE WAS KILLED.
ALTHOUGH WE HAVE NO TRACE OF THE MURDERER, WE WON'T GIVE UP TRYING TO FIND HIM - BUT THAT WON'T BRING BACK OUR BELOVED WILLIAM.

ONLY YOU CAN COMFORT ELIZABETH. SHE WEEPS CONSTANTLY AND BLAMES HERSELF FOR WILLIAM'S DEATH.
PLEASE COME HOME TO US, VICTOR.
YOUR FATHER,
ALPHONSE FRANKENSTEIN.
MY DEAR FRANKENSTEIN, WHAT ARE YOU GOING TO DO?
I'LL GO TO GENEVA, IMMEDIATELY.
I SAID GOODBYE TO MY FRIEND, AND AS I GOT CLOSER TO HOME, I WAS OVERCOME WITH GRIEF AND FEAR.

ALTHOUGH IT WAS DARK WHEN I REACHED GENEVA, I WAS UNABLE TO REST.
I DECIDED TO VISIT THE SPOT WHERE WILLIAM WAS MURDERED, AND I HAD TO TRAVEL BY BOAT TO GET THERE.
LIGHTNING FLASHED TOWARD US, AND THUNDER CRASHED OVERHEAD.
KRAKKA-DOOM!
WILLIAM, DEAR ANGEL!
THIS IS YOUR FUNERAL!

AS I SAID THESE WORDS, I SAW A FIGURE IN THE GLOOM.
A FLASH OF LIGHTNING REVEALED THAT IT WAS THE WRETCH...
...THE FILTHY DEMON TO WHOM I HAD GIVEN LIFE.
WHAT WAS HE DOING THERE? COULD HE BE THE MURDERER OF MY BROTHER?
NOTHING HUMAN COULD HAVE HARMED THAT FAIR CHILD.
HE WAS THE MURDERER!
I COULDN'T FOLLOW HIM - HE DISAPPEARED AMONG THE ROCKS OF MOUNT SALÊVE.

HE SOON REACHED THE SUMMIT...
...AND DISAPPEARED.

IT WAS FIVE IN THE MORNING WHEN I ARRIVED AT MY FATHER'S HOUSE.

I WENT STRAIGHT TO THE LIBRARY.

Caroline Beaufort-Frankens
I HADN'T BEEN HERE FOR SIX YEARS.

MY DEAREST VICTOR!

ERNEST!
AH! I WISH YOU HAD COME THREE MONTHS AGO.
THIS IS SUCH A SAD TIME,
BUT I'M SURE YOU BEING HERE WILL MAKE OUR FATHER AND ELIZABETH FEEL HAPPIER.

ELIZABETH...?
SHE BLAMED HERSELF FOR THE MURDER.
BUT, SINCE THE MURDERER HAS BEEN FOUND...

BUT HOW?!? I SAW HIM LAST NIGHT, AND HE WAS FREE! HOW WAS HE CAUGHT?
I DON'T KNOW WHAT YOU MEAN!
OUR MISERY IS COMPLETE - THE EVIDENCE SHOWS THAT IT WAS JUSTINE MORITZ!
SURELY NO ONE BELIEVES THAT?
NOT AT FIRST, BUT SHE HAS ACTED VERY STRANGELY LATELY. SHE IS APPEARING IN COURT TODAY.
ONE OF THE SERVANTS FOUND THE LOCKET THAT WAS STOLEN FROM WILLIAM, IN JUSTINE'S POCKET.
YOU ARE ALL MISTAKEN.
I KNOW THE MURDERER, AND IT IS NOT JUSTINE.

PAPA! VICTOR SAYS THAT JUSTINE IS INNOCENT!
IF SHE IS, THEN GOD FORBID THAT SHE IS FOUND GUILTY.
DEAR COUSIN, YOU FILL ME WITH HOPE. I'LL NEVER BE HAPPY AGAIN IF JUSTINE IS CONDEMNED.
DON'T WORRY - THE COURT SHALL PROVE THAT SHE IS INNOCENT.

VOLUME I
CHAPTER VIII
A THOUSAND TIMES I THOUGHT ABOUT CONFESSING TO THE CRIME - BUT THEY'D HAVE THOUGHT THAT I WAS A MADMAN.

JUSTINE SEEMED CALM AND CONFIDENT IN HER INNOCENCE AS SHE ENTERED THE COURT.
A TEAR CAME INTO HER EYE WHEN SHE SAW US.

JUSTINE HAD BEEN OUT ON THE NIGHT OF THE MURDER, AND EARLY IN THE MORNING SHE WAS SEEN BY A MARKET-WOMAN, CLOSE TO WHERE WILLIAM'S BODY WAS FOUND.
I ASKED HER WHAT SHE WAS DOING, BUT SHE SEEMED CONFUSED.
JUSTINE WAS CALLED TO DEFEND HERSELF. SHE WAS CLOSE TO TEARS, AND HER VOICE WAS SHAKY.
I AM INNOCENT.
I SPENT THE EVENING AT MY AUNT'S HOUSE. ON THE WAY BACK, A MAN ASKED ME IF I HAD SEEN THE CHILD WHO WAS LOST.
I SPENT MANY HOURS LOOKING FOR HIM.
I TRIED TO RETURN TO GENEVA, BUT IT WAS SO LATE THAT THE GATES WERE SHUT --
-- SO I SPENT THE REST OF THE NIGHT IN A BARN.
THIS PICTURE WAS FOUND IN JUSTINE'S POCKET.
IT'S THE SAME ONE THAT WILLIAM WAS WEARING BEFORE HE WENT MISSING.
A MURMUR OF HORROR FILLED THE COURT.
AT DAWN, I WAS WOKEN BY THE SOUND OF FOOTSTEPS. I DECIDED TO LOOK FOR THE MISSING CHILD AGAIN.
I WAS STILL WEARY FROM HAVING HAD LITTLE SLEEP WHEN I MET WITH THE MARKET-WOMAN.
I DON'T KNOW HOW THE PICTURE GOT INTO MY POCKET. I KNOW HOW BAD THAT LOOKS FOR ME, BUT I CANNOT EXPLAIN IT.
IT'S UP TO THE COURT TO DECIDE WHAT HAPPENS TO ME NOW.

SEVERAL WITNESSES WERE CALLED TO HER DEFENSE, AND ELIZABETH EVEN SPOKE TO THE COURT DIRECTLY, BUT OPINION WENT AGAINST JUSTINE.
IN THE MORNING, I WENT TO THE COURT TO HEAR THE VERDICT: JUSTINE WAS FOUND GUILTY.
...BUT SHE HAS CONFESSED!
HOW CAN I TRUST ANYONE AGAIN?
I'LL SEE HER, EVEN THOUGH SHE'S GUILTY.
OH, JUSTINE!
WHY DID YOU DO IT??
I THOUGHT YOU WERE INNOCENT!
I DID CONFESS, BUT THAT WAS A LIE! I AM INNOCENT!
EVER SINCE I CAME HERE, I'VE BEEN THREATENED AND MENACED, UNTIL I ALMOST BEGAN TO THINK THAT I WAS THE MURDERING MONSTER.
WHAT ELSE COULD I DO?
OH, JUSTINE! FORGIVE ME FOR NOT TRUSTING YOU.
DO NOT FEAR - I WILL PROVE YOUR INNOCENCE.
YOU SHALL NOT DIE!
I'M NOT AFRAID OF DYING;
I CAN GO IN PEACE, KNOWING THAT YOU BOTH BELIEVE I'M INNOCENT.
THE POOR SUFFERER TRIED TO COMFORT US ALL - BUT I, THE TRUE MURDERER, FELT NO CONSOLATION IN MY HEART...

...AND IN THE MORNING, JUSTINE DIED.
I SAW THOSE I LOVED CRYING OVER THE GRAVES OF WILLIAM AND JUSTINE - THE FIRST VICTIMS OF MY CREATION.
VOLUME II
CHAPTER I
I HAD STARTED OFF WITH GOOD INTENTIONS, TO BENEFIT MY FELLOW BEINGS. NOW ALL WAS RUINED. FULL OF GUILT, I NEEDED TO BE ALONE.
I HAD BROUGHT ABOUT TERRIBLE EVILS, AND I LIVED IN FEAR OF THE MONSTER STRIKING AGAIN.
WHEN I THINK ABOUT THE MISERABLE DEATH OF JUSTINE, I FEEL AS IF I'M STANDING ON THE EDGE OF A CLIFF, WITH THOUSANDS OF PEOPLE WAITING TO PUSH ME OFF.
WILLIAM AND JUSTINE WERE KILLED, AND THE MURDERER WALKS ABOUT THE WORLD FREE.
WITH MY FATHER'S HEALTH SHAKEN, AND ELIZABETH SO SAD, I COULDN'T COPE ANYMORE; MY SOUL DROVE ME TO SUDDENLY LEAVE.

VOLUME II
CHAPTER II
TRYING TO FORGET MY SORROWS, I HEADED FOR THE ALPINE VALLEYS.
I DECIDED TO CLIMB TO THE SUMMIT OF MONTANVERT.
SEEING THE GLACIER THERE HAD A GREAT EFFECT ON ME WHEN I FIRST SAW IT, YEARS AGO.
THE CLIMB WAS HAZARDOUS, AND MY SURROUNDINGS WERE OFTEN GLOOMY - BUT THAT DIDN'T STOP ME.

IT WAS NEARLY NOON WHEN I ARRIVED AT THE TOP OF THE MOUNTAIN. I GAZED AT THE WONDERFUL VIEW.
MY HEART SWELLED WITH JOY.
WANDERING SPIRITS, ALLOW ME THIS HAPPINESS, OR TAKE ME AWAY FROM THE JOYS OF LIFE!
AS I SPOKE, I SUDDENLY SAW THE FIGURE OF A HUGE MAN COMING TOWARD ME AT SUPERHUMAN SPEED.
IT WAS THE WRETCH THAT I HAD CREATED. I SHOOK WITH ANGER AND HORROR, WAITING TO FIGHT HIM IN MORTAL COMBAT!

DEVIL, AREN'T YOU SCARED OF ME?
LEAVE, VILE INSECT!
OR STAY AND I'LL TRAMPLE YOU TO DUST!
OH, IF ONLY KILLING YOU WOULD BRING BACK THOSE VICTIMS YOU HAVE MURDERED!
I EXPECTED THIS.
ALL MEN HATE THE WRETCHED -
AND YOU, MY CREATOR, DETEST ME, AND WANT TO KILL ME.
DO YOUR DUTY TO ME, AND I WILL LEAVE YOU AND ALL MANKIND ALONE - BUT REFUSE, AND I SHALL MURDER YOUR REMAINING FRIENDS.
YOU MONSTER!
LUNGE!
WRETCHED DEVIL!
I'LL PUT OUT THE SPARK OF LIFE THAT I SO STUPIDLY GAVE YOU!

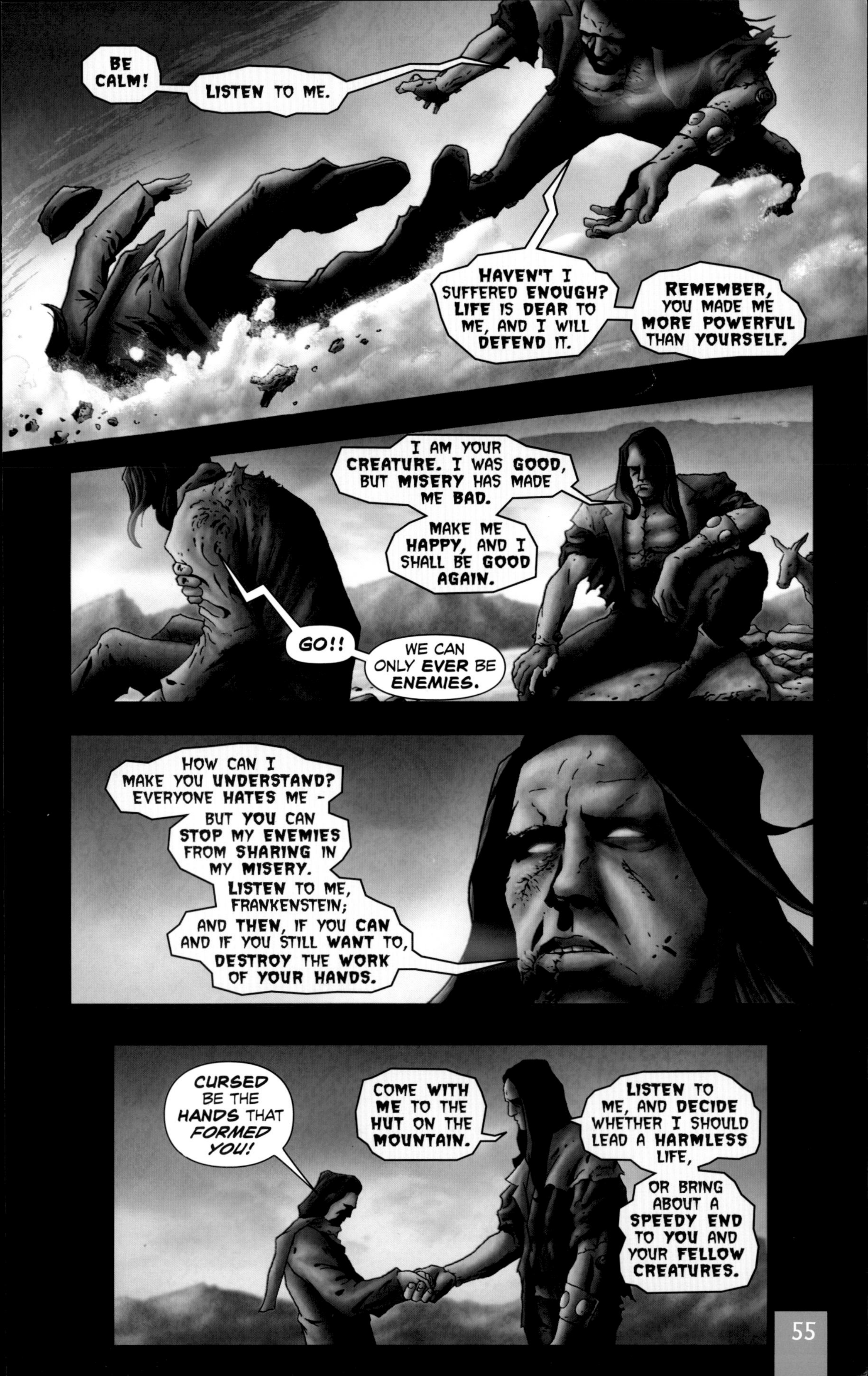
BE CALM!
LISTEN TO ME.
HAVEN'T I SUFFERED ENOUGH? LIFE IS DEAR TO ME, AND I WILL DEFEND IT.
REMEMBER, YOU MADE ME MORE POWERFUL THAN YOURSELF.
I AM YOUR CREATURE. I WAS GOOD, BUT MISERY HAS MADE ME BAD.
MAKE ME HAPPY, AND I SHALL BE GOOD AGAIN.
GO!!
WE CAN ONLY EVER BE ENEMIES.
HOW CAN I MAKE YOU UNDERSTAND? EVERYONE HATES ME -
BUT YOU CAN STOP MY ENEMIES FROM SHARING IN MY MISERY.
LISTEN TO ME, FRANKENSTEIN;
AND THEN, IF YOU CAN AND IF YOU STILL WANT TO, DESTROY THE WORK OF YOUR HANDS.
CURSED BE THE HANDS THAT FORMED YOU!
COME WITH ME TO THE HUT ON THE MOUNTAIN.
LISTEN TO ME, AND DECIDE WHETHER I SHOULD LEAD A HARMLESS LIFE,
OR BRING ABOUT A SPEEDY END TO YOU AND YOUR FELLOW CREATURES.

I DECIDED TO **LISTEN** TO HIS **TALE.**

FOR THE **FIRST TIME**, I **REALIZED** THAT, AS **CREATOR** OF THIS **CREATURE**, I HAD AN **OBLIGATION** TO HIM.

VOLUME II CHAPTER III

I **STRUGGLE** TO **REMEMBER** MY **FIRST DAYS** - IT TOOK A **WHILE** FOR ME TO **RECOGNIZE** MY **SENSES.**

I WENT TO THE **FOREST** NEAR **INGOLSTADT. THERE** I FOUND **BERRIES** TO **EAT**, AND **WATER** TO **DRINK.**

FOOD WAS SCARCE, AND I OFTEN SPENT THE WHOLE DAY SEARCHING FOR A FEW ACORNS.
I LONGED FOR FOOD AND SHELTER - THEN, I FOUND A SMALL HUT.
THE DOOR WAS OPEN. INSIDE, AN OLD MAN WAS PREPARING HIS BREAKFAST.
HE SAW ME AND RAN AWAY, SCREAMING.
I WAS SURPRISED BY HIS REACTION - BUT I WAS FASCINATED BY THE HUT: HERE WAS A PLACE WHERE THE SNOW AND RAIN COULDN'T GET IN.

I GREEDILY ATE HIS BREAKFAST AND FELL ASLEEP IN THE STRAW.

IT WAS NOON WHEN I AWOKE. DRAWN BY THE WARMTH OF THE SUN, I CONTINUED MY JOURNEY.

SEVERAL HOURS LATER, I ARRIVED AT A VILLAGE.

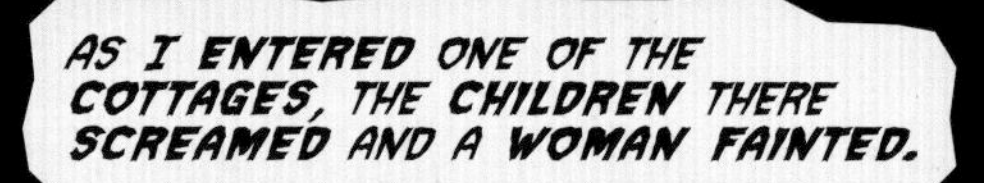
AS I ENTERED ONE OF THE COTTAGES, THE CHILDREN THERE SCREAMED AND A WOMAN FAINTED.

THE WHOLE VILLAGE TURNED OUT AGAINST ME AND ATTACKED ME WITH STONES AND WEAPONS UNTIL I ESCAPED TO THE OPEN COUNTRY.

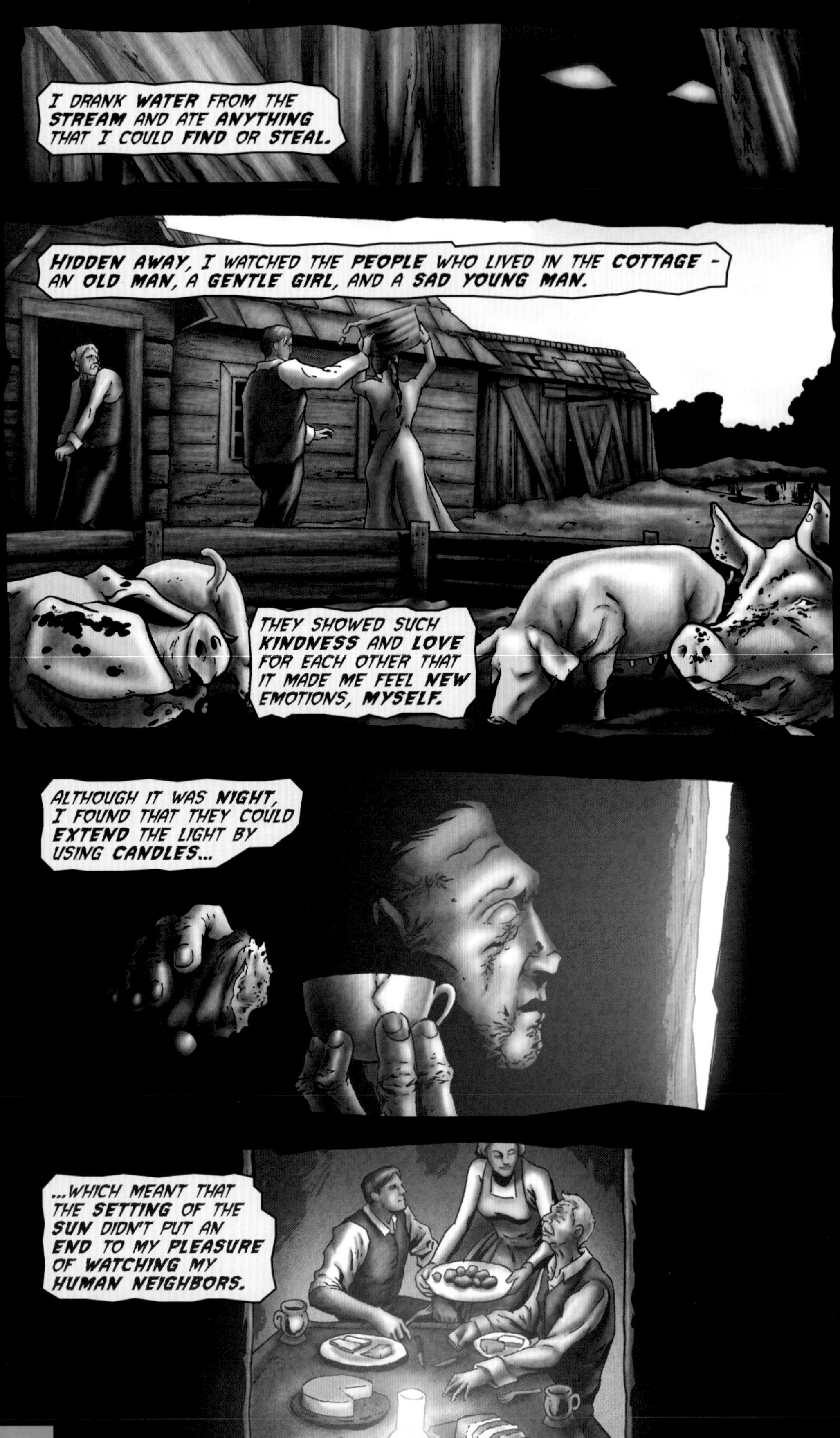
I DRANK WATER FROM THE STREAM AND ATE ANYTHING THAT I COULD FIND OR STEAL.
HIDDEN AWAY, I WATCHED THE PEOPLE WHO LIVED IN THE COTTAGE - AN OLD MAN, A GENTLE GIRL, AND A SAD YOUNG MAN.
THEY SHOWED SUCH KINDNESS AND LOVE FOR EACH OTHER THAT IT MADE ME FEEL NEW EMOTIONS, MYSELF.
ALTHOUGH IT WAS NIGHT, I FOUND THAT THEY COULD EXTEND THE LIGHT BY USING CANDLES...
...WHICH MEANT THAT THE SETTING OF THE SUN DIDN'T PUT AN END TO MY PLEASURE OF WATCHING MY HUMAN NEIGHBORS.

VOLUME II
CHAPTER IV
I SOON REALIZED THAT THE OLD MAN WAS BLIND. THE YOUNG PEOPLE SHOWED MUCH LOVE FOR HIM.
I LONGED TO JOIN THEM, BUT I DARED NOT.
THEY WERE NOT ENTIRELY HAPPY, ALTHOUGH I COULDN'T SEE WHAT MADE THEM SO MISERABLE.
A WHILE LATER, I DISCOVERED ONE OF THE CAUSES: POVERTY.
THEY REGULARLY WENT HUNGRY, ESPECIALLY THE YOUNGER COTTAGERS WHO OFTEN PLACED FOOD BEFORE THE OLD MAN AND HAD NONE THEMSELVES.
WHEN I REALIZED THIS, I STOPPED TAKING THEIR FOOD AND SATISFIED MYSELF WITH BERRIES, NUTS AND ROOTS FROM THE NEARBY WOOD.
I ALSO LEARNED HOW TO USE THEIR TOOLS SO THAT I COULD HELP THEM WITH THEIR TASKS.
AT NIGHT I WOULD OFTEN BRING FIREWOOD FOR THEM - ENOUGH FOR SEVERAL DAYS.

I DISCOVERED THAT THE WORDS THEY SPOKE TO EACH OTHER WERE IMPORTANT - AND, SLOWLY, I WORKED OUT THE NAMES THAT THEY GAVE TO FAMILIAR OBJECTS.
I LEARNED SIMPLE WORDS AS WELL AS THE NAMES OF THE COTTAGERS THEMSELVES.
THE OLD MAN WAS "FATHER".
THE GIRL WAS "SISTER", OR "AGATHA".
THE YOUNG MAN WAS "FELIX", "BROTHER", OR "SON".
I WAS SO HAPPY WHEN I DISCOVERED WHAT THESE SOUNDS MEANT, AND THAT I WAS ABLE TO SAY THEM. I MADE OUT OTHER WORDS, TOO - SUCH AS "GOOD", "DEAREST" AND "UNHAPPY".

ALL WINTER I STUDIED THE COTTAGERS TO LEARN THEIR WAYS. I SHARED THEIR JOYS AND THEIR SORROWS.
FELIX WAS THE SADDEST OF THE THREE.
EVEN IN SUCH POVERTY, I SAW HIM BRING HAPPINESS TO HIS SISTER WITH THE GIFT OF A WHITE FLOWER TAKEN FROM THE SNOWY GROUND.
THE COTTAGERS WERE SO BEAUTIFUL, AND I WAS SHOCKED AND TERRIFIED TO SEE HOW UGLY I WAS WHEN I SAW MY REFLECTION IN A POOL.
I DIDN'T BELIEVE IT AT FIRST - BUT I SOON REALIZED THAT I WAS TRULY A MONSTER!
EACH DAY WAS MUCH LIKE ANOTHER.
I SLEPT DURING THE DAY AND WORKED FOR THE COTTAGERS ONCE THEY HAD GONE TO SLEEP. I WOULD CLEAR THEIR PATH OF SNOW AND COLLECT FOOD AND FUEL FOR THEM. THEY THOUGHT IT WAS A "GOOD SPIRIT" THAT DID SUCH WORK FOR THEM, BECAUSE THEY NEVER SAW ME.
I THOUGHT THAT I COULD MAKE THEM HAPPY AND WIN THEIR FAVOR. TO DO THIS, I NEEDED TO LEARN THEIR LANGUAGE.

VOLUME II
CHAPTER V
SPRING CAME, AND YET FELIX WAS SADDER THAN EVER.
THEN, HE HAD A VISITOR.
FELIX?
MY SWEET ARABIAN!
THIS VISITOR MADE FELIX SO VERY HAPPY.
SHE DIDN'T SEEM TO UNDERSTAND HIM, BUT SMILED A LOT. THEY CALLED HER "SAFIE".
JOY SEEMED TO TAKE THE PLACE OF SADNESS. I WATCHED AND LISTENED CLOSELY AS FELIX TAUGHT SAFIE THEIR LANGUAGE.
SHE AND I BOTH IMPROVED RAPIDLY, AND IN THE SPACE OF TWO MONTHS I COULD UNDERSTAND MOST OF THEIR WORDS.
I ALSO LISTENED AS THEY STUDIED BOOKS, SUCH AS 'RUINS OF EMPIRES', WHICH SHOWED ME THE MANNERS, GOVERNMENTS AND RELIGIONS OF DIFFERENT COUNTRIES.

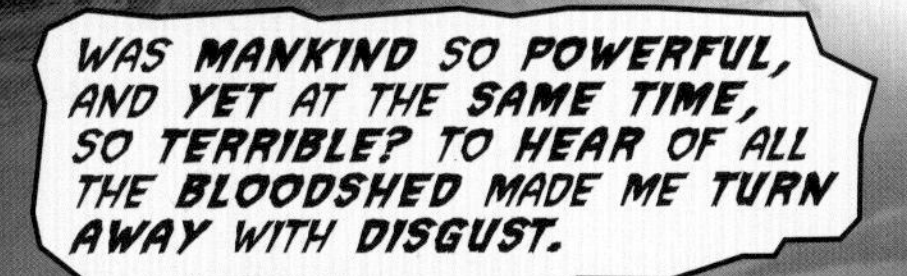
WAS MANKIND SO POWERFUL, AND YET AT THE SAME TIME, SO TERRIBLE? TO HEAR OF ALL THE BLOODSHED MADE ME TURN AWAY WITH DISGUST.
AND WHAT WAS I?
I KNEW NOTHING OF MY CREATION OR OF MY CREATOR. I WAS UGLY; AND NOT EVEN OF THE SAME MAKING AS MAN.

I LEARNED ABOUT BIRTH AND FAMILIES.
BUT WHERE WERE MY FRIENDS AND FAMILY?
NO PARENTS HAD WATCHED OVER ME AS A CHILD -
WHAT WAS I?

WHO WERE THIS FAMILY?
THE DE LACEYS - FROM PARIS.
THEY CAME FROM A GOOD FRENCH FAMILY WHO HAD BEEN RUINED BY SAFIE'S FATHER.
HE WAS A TURKISH MERCHANT, THROWN INTO PRISON BY THE FRENCH GOVERNMENT AND CONDEMNED TO DEATH.
FELIX, WHO HAD BEEN PRESENT AT THE TRIAL, PROMISED TO FREE HIM...
...AND WHEN HE SAW THE MERCHANT'S BEAUTIFUL DAUGHTER, HE AGREED WITH THE TURK THAT SAFIE SHOULD BE HIS REWARD.
FELIX LED THE FUGITIVES THROUGH FRANCE. SECRETLY, THE TURK HATED THE IDEA OF HIS DAUGHTER MARRYING A CHRISTIAN, AND SO HE HATCHED A PLAN TO DECEIVE FELIX AND TAKE HIS DAUGHTER WITH HIM.

FELIX'S PLOT WAS SOON DISCOVERED, AND HIS FATHER AND SISTER WERE THROWN INTO PRISON.
NEWS OF THIS REACHED FELIX, WHO MADE ARRANGEMENTS WITH THE TURK FOR SAFIE AND RETURNED QUICKLY TO PARIS.
FELIX TURNED HIMSELF IN, HOPING THAT DE LACY AND AGATHA WOULD BE FREED.
INSTEAD, THEY WERE ALL IMPRISONED FOR FIVE MONTHS, AFTER WHICH THEY WERE STRIPPED OF THEIR FORTUNE AND SENT AWAY FROM FRANCE FOREVER.
HEARING THAT FELIX HAD LOST HIS FORTUNE, THE TURK TOLD HIS DAUGHTER TO STOP ALL THOUGHTS OF HER LOVER. SAFIE WAS OUTRAGED.
HER FATHER LEFT FOR TURKEY, LEAVING SAFIE ALONE. FINDING SOME OF HER FATHER'S PAPERS SHE FOUND OUT THAT FELIX NOW LIVED IN GERMANY AND SHE DECIDED TO GO THERE TO LIVE WITH HER EXILED LOVER.
VOLUME II
CHAPTER VII
ONE NIGHT, IN THE WOOD, I FOUND SOME BOOKS IN A LEATHER CASE.

ONE OF THE BOOKS WAS 'PARADISE LOST'.
I WAS JUST LIKE ADAM - NOT LINKED TO ANY OTHER BEING IN EXISTENCE. YET HE WAS PERFECT AND HAPPY -
WHEREAS I WAS HIDEOUS AND SAD.
MUCH EARLIER, I HAD DISCOVERED YOUR JOURNAL OF MY CREATION. IT WAS IN THE POCKET OF YOUR CLOTHES THAT I TOOK FROM YOUR APARTMENT.
NOW THAT I WAS ABLE TO READ, I BEGAN TO STUDY IT.
Paradise Lost
HERE IT IS. EVERY LITTLE DETAIL OF MY FOUL ORIGIN.
READING IT MADE ME SICK.
WHY DID YOU MAKE A MONSTER, ONE SO HIDEOUS THAT EVEN YOU TURNED AWAY IN DISGUST?
GOD MADE MAN IN HIS OWN IMAGE, BUT MY FORM IS A FILTHY TYPE OF YOURS.
EVEN SATAN HAD HIS COMPANIONS, BUT I AM ALONE AND HATED.

MY CREATOR HAD ABANDONED ME - AND IN THE BITTERNESS OF MY HEART, I CURSED HIM.
I WAITED FOR THE RIGHT MOMENT TO INTRODUCE MYSELF TO THE COTTAGERS.
MONTHS PASSED; THEN, ONE DAY, WHEN THE OLD MAN WAS LEFT ALONE, I APPROACHED THE DOOR OF THE COTTAGE...
KNOCK KNOCK
WHO'S THERE? COME IN.
PARDON ME - I'M A TRAVELER IN NEED OF REST.
COME IN, BUT AS I'M BLIND, I CAN'T OFFER YOU ANY FOOD.
ALL I WANT IS WARMTH AND REST.

I AM AN UNFORTUNATE AND DESERTED CREATURE. I HAVE NO RELATION OR FRIEND IN THE WORLD.
I AM NOW GOING TO CLAIM THE PROTECTION OF SOME FRIENDS - SOME KIND PEOPLE WHO HAVE NEVER SEEN ME.
IF I FAIL, I'LL BE CAST OUT FOREVER.
RELY ON YOUR HOPES AND DO NOT DESPAIR.
BUT THEIR EYES ARE CLOUDED -
WHERE THEY SHOULD SEE A KIND FRIEND, THEY ONLY SEE A HORRIBLE MONSTER.
ALTHOUGH I SHOW THEM KINDNESS, THEY BELIEVE THAT I WISH TO HARM THEM.
WHERE DO THEY LIVE?
NEAR HERE.
PERHAPS I CAN HELP. WHAT ARE THE NAMES OF THOSE FRIENDS?
AT THAT MOMENT, I HEARD THE FOOTSTEPS OF THE OTHER COTTAGERS...

NOW IS THE TIME! SAVE AND PROTECT ME!
YOU AND YOUR FAMILY ARE THE FRIENDS I SEEK! DON'T DESERT ME!

WHO ARE YOU?

I CANNOT DESCRIBE THEIR HORROR WHEN THEY SAW ME.

AGATHA FAINTED; SAFIE RAN AWAY, AND FELIX TORE ME AWAY FROM HIS FATHER.

CRACK!
HE THREW ME TO THE GROUND. I COULD HAVE TORN HIM APART - BUT MY HEART SANK WITH SADNESS, AND I STOPPED MYSELF.
OVERCOME BY PAIN, I LEFT THE COTTAGE AND ESCAPED UNSEEN TO MY HOVEL.
VOLUME II
CHAPTER VIII
THE FAMILY ABANDONED THE COTTAGE.
IN MY RAGE, I LIT THE DRY BRANCH OF A TREE, AND THE COTTAGE WAS SOON ON FIRE.
AND NOW, WHERE SHOULD I GO?
I LEARNED FROM YOUR PAPERS THAT YOU WERE MY CREATOR, AND THAT YOU WERE FROM GENEVA...
...SO THAT'S WHERE I HEADED.

MY TRAVELS WERE LONG. I RESTED DURING THE DAY AND TRAVELED AT NIGHT WHEN I WAS SURE I WOULDN'T BE SEEN.
ONE MORNING, AS I WALKED THROUGH A DEEP WOOD, I DECIDED TO CONTINUE AFTER SUNRISE. IT WAS A BEAUTIFUL SPRING DAY.
HEARING VOICES, I HID. A YOUNG GIRL RAN ALONG THE SIDE OF THE RIVER.
SHE SLIPPED AND FELL INTO THE RAPID STREAM!

I RUSHED TO SAVE HER...
...AND DRAGGED HER BACK TO THE SHORE.
SHE WASN'T MOVING, AND I TRIED EVERYTHING TO BRING HER BACK TO LIFE. SUDDENLY, A MAN DARTED TOWARD ME...

TEARING THE GIRL FROM MY ARMS, HE RAN BACK INTO THE WOODS; I FOLLOWED.
WHEN HE SAW ME DRAWING NEAR, HE AIMED HIS GUN AT ME...
...AND FIRED!
BLAMM!
KRAKK!
ARRGH!
I SANK TO THE GROUND, AND THE MAN ESCAPED INTO THE WOOD.
I'D SAVED SOMEONE'S LIFE, AND AS A REWARD, I HAD A SHATTERING WOUND.
IN GREAT PAIN, I VOWED ETERNAL HATRED AND VENGEANCE TO ALL MANKIND.

AFTER SOME WEEKS, MY WOUND HEALED; I CONTINUED MY JOURNEY, AND IN TWO MONTHS, I APPROACHED GENEVA.

I DON'T WANT TO HURT YOU; LISTEN TO ME.
LET ME GO!
MONSTER! UGLY WRETCH!
YOU WISH TO EAT ME!
LET ME GO - OR I WILL TELL PAPA!
YOU WILL NEVER SEE YOUR FATHER AGAIN - YOU MUST COME WITH ME.
HIDEOUS MONSTER! LET ME GO!
MY FATHER IS MONSIEUR FRANKENSTEIN
- HE WILL PUNISH YOU!

FRANKENSTEIN!
YOU BELONG TO MY ENEMY!
THEN YOU WILL BE MY FIRST VICTIM!

THE CHILD STRUGGLED. I GRASPED HIS THROAT TO SILENCE HIM...
...AND IN A MOMENT HE WAS DEAD.

I TOO CAN CREATE SORROW! THIS DEATH SHALL TORMENT AND DESTROY MY ENEMY!
AROUND HIS NECK, I SAW A PICTURE OF A BEAUTIFUL WOMAN.
I WOULD NEVER KNOW THE DELIGHTS SUCH BEAUTY COULD BRING.

I LOOKED FOR SOMEWHERE TO HIDE AND ENTERED A BARN.
THERE, I FOUND A YOUNG WOMAN SLEEPING ON SOME STRAW.
SHE WOULD NEVER SMILE AT ME.
WAKE UP - YOUR LOVER IS NEAR. AWAKE, MY BELOVED.
F
SHE STIRRED - I WAS FRIGHTENED THAT SHE WOULD WAKE AND REALIZE THAT I WAS THE MURDERER.
I DECIDED THAT NOT I, BUT SHE SHOULD SUFFER!
HER LOVELINESS WAS THE SOURCE OF MY CRIME - AND SO THE PUNISHMENT WILL BE HERS, TOO.
I PLACED THE PICTURE IN ONE OF THE FOLDS OF HER DRESS...
...AND FLED.

FOR DAYS I STAYED CLOSE TO THE SCENE OF THE MURDER. I WANDERED TO THESE MOUNTAINS - WITH AN OBSESSION THAT ONLY YOU CAN SATISFY.
YOU MUST NOW PROMISE TO DO AS I ASK.
I AM ALONE AND MISERABLE.
MAN HATES ME --
-- SO YOU MUST CREATE A WOMAN WHO IS JUST LIKE ME; SHE WILL NOT DENY HERSELF TO ME.
VOLUME II
CHAPTER IX
ONLY YOU CAN DO THIS - YOU MUST NOT REFUSE.
NO!
YOU CAN TORTURE ME, BUT I'LL NEVER DO THAT!
I AM ONLY EVIL BECAUSE I AM MISERABLE.
LET ME BE GRATEFUL TO YOU FOR JUST THIS ONE THING!
DO NOT DENY ME THIS!

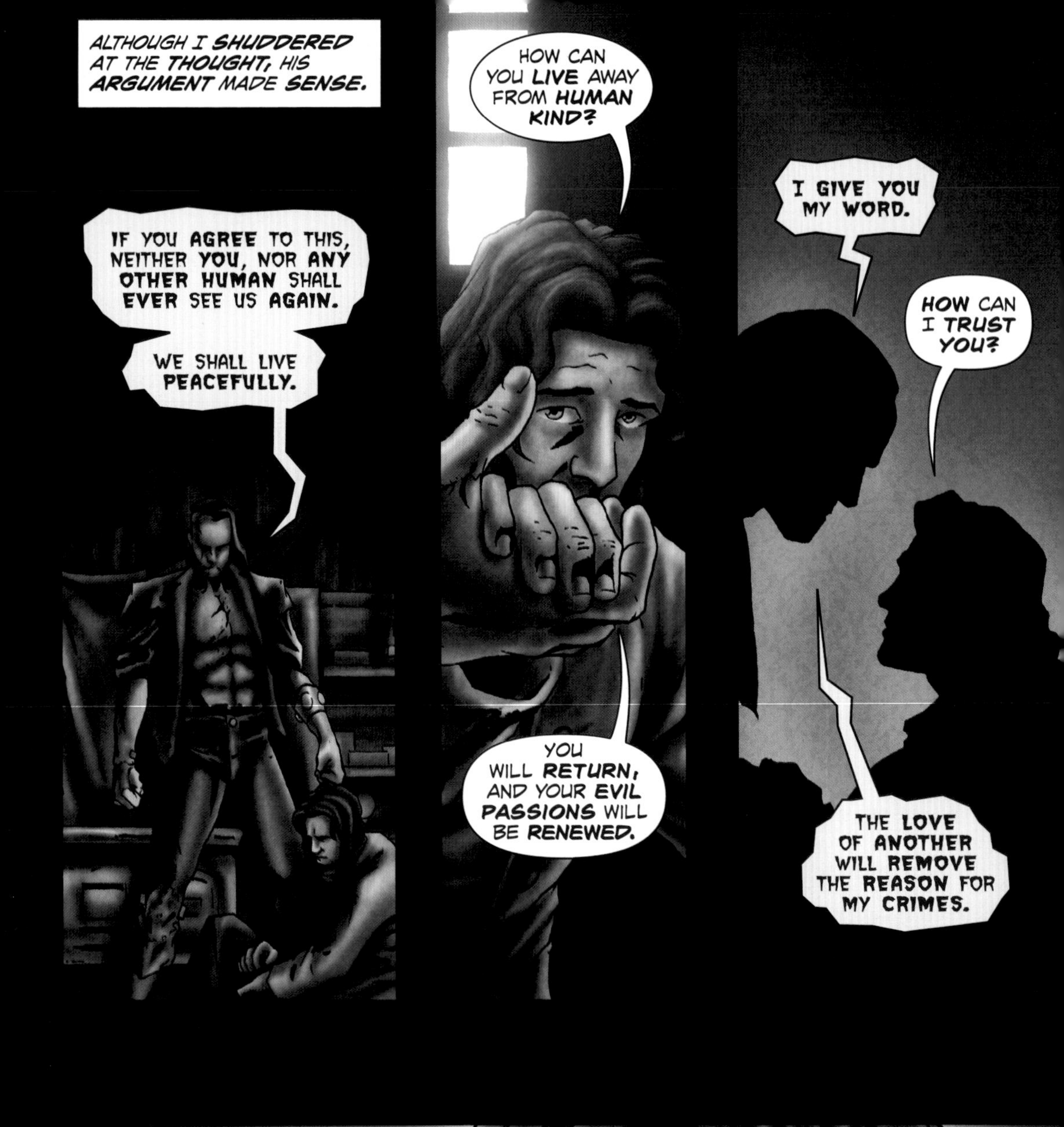
ALTHOUGH I SHUDDERED AT THE THOUGHT, HIS ARGUMENT MADE SENSE.
IF YOU AGREE TO THIS, NEITHER YOU, NOR ANY OTHER HUMAN SHALL EVER SEE US AGAIN.
WE SHALL LIVE PEACEFULLY.
HOW CAN YOU LIVE AWAY FROM HUMAN KIND?
YOU WILL RETURN, AND YOUR EVIL PASSIONS WILL BE RENEWED.
I GIVE YOU MY WORD.
HOW CAN I TRUST YOU?
THE LOVE OF ANOTHER WILL REMOVE THE REASON FOR MY CRIMES.

I'LL DO IT,
AS LONG AS YOU PROMISE TO LEAVE EUROPE FOREVER AND NEVER VISIT ANY AREA INHABITED BY MAN.

RETURNED HOME TO MY
AMILY IN GENEVA.

Y APPEARANCE ALARMED
HEM, AND I FOUND IT HARD
O SPEAK; YET I LOVED
HEM WITH ALL MY HEART. TO
AVE THEM, I DEDICATED
YSELF TO THIS MOST
ORRIBLE TASK.

VOLUME III CHAPTER I

IN THAT CASE, WE SHALL ALL BE HAPPY. TELL ME, THEN - WOULD YOU OBJECT TO AN IMMEDIATE MARRIAGE?
I WAS UNABLE TO ANSWER MY FATHER.
I COULDN'T THINK ABOUT MARRYING ELIZABETH UNTIL I HAD COMPLETED THE TASK FOR THE MONSTER.

THE MONSTER MUST DEPART WITH HIS MATE BEFORE I COULD ENJOY MY FUTURE LIFE IN PEACE.

I NEEDED TO TRAVEL TO ENGLAND TO GAIN NEW INFORMATION FOR MY TASK. IT WAS ALSO IMPORTANT FOR ME TO BE AWAY FROM ALL I LOVED.
THESE MATTERS DECIDED THE ANSWER I GAVE TO MY FATHER.

I MADE MY FATHER AGREE TO THE TRIP.
HE INSISTED THAT I TAKE HENRY CLERVAL WITH ME.

ALTHOUGH I NEEDED TO BE ALONE FOR MY WORK, CLERVAL'S COMPANY WOULD SAVE ME FROM HOURS OF LONELY, MADDENING THOUGHT.
HAVING HIM THERE MIGHT EVEN STOP THE MONSTER FROM WANTING TO VISIT ME.

I WAS TO MARRY ELIZABETH WHEN I RETURNED - A PEACEFUL LIFE WITH MY BELOVED WAS THE ONE REWARD FOR MY HORRID TASK.

BUT WHAT IF HE DIDN'T FOLLOW ME? HE COULD ATTACK MY FAMILY WHILE I WAS AWAY IN ENGLAND.
NO - HE SAID THAT HE WOULD FOLLOW ME WHEREVER I WENT. MY FAMILY AND FRIENDS WERE SAFE.

VOLUME III
CHAPTER II
WE DECIDED TO STAY IN LONDON FOR A FEW MONTHS.
YEARS AGO, I WOULD HAVE THOROUGHLY ENJOYED SUCH A JOURNEY...
...BUT A SICKENING MENACE HAD ENTERED MY LIFE.
THIS IS LIVING! BUT WHY ARE YOU SO MISERABLE, FRANKENSTEIN?
HAVING CLERVAL WITH ME LIFTED MY SPIRITS.
CLERVAL WANTED TO MEET PEOPLE OF GENIUS AND TALENT IN LONDON. THIS WAS NOT IMPORTANT TO ME.
MY PURPOSE WAS TO OBTAIN THE INFORMATION I NEEDED TO COMPLETE MY TASK.
TAKING MY LETTERS OF INTRODUCTION, I SOUGHT OUT THE MOST LEARNED OF MEN.

I ONLY VISITED THESE PEOPLE FOR INFORMATION.
UNLIKE CLERVAL, I COULDN'T BRING MYSELF TO ENJOY THEIR COMPANY.
CLERVAL WAS JUST AS I USED TO BE: ANXIOUS, INQUISITIVE, AND KEEN TO ACCOMPLISH SOMETHING.
HE WANTED TO VISIT INDIA SO THAT HE COULD LEARN ABOUT TRADE THERE.
HE WAS ALWAYS BUSY; I OFTEN TOLD HIM I HAD TO GO SOMEWHERE ELSE - JUST SO THAT I COULD BE ALONE.
I NOW ALSO BEGAN TO COLLECT THE MATERIALS THAT I NEEDED...
...FOR MY NEW CREATION.

WE RECEIVED AN INVITATION TO VISIT AN OLD FRIEND IN SCOTLAND. CLERVAL EAGERLY ACCEPTED; ALTHOUGH I HATED THE IDEA OF MEETING PEOPLE, I LONGED TO SEE MOUNTAINS AGAIN.
ON THE WAY WE VISITED WINDSOR, OXFORD, MATLOCK, AND THE CUMBERLAND LAKES.
I TOOK MY INSTRUMENTS AND MATERIALS SO THAT I COULD FINISH MY WORK IN THE SCOTTISH HIGHLANDS.
CLERVAL LOVED EDINBURGH - BUT I WAS EAGER TO GET TO THE END OF MY JOURNEY.
SOMETIMES I FELT THAT THE MONSTER MIGHT MURDER MY FRIEND SO THAT HE MIGHT REFOCUS MY EFFORTS.
IT WAS AS IF I HAD COMMITTED SOME CRIME. I WAS GUILTLESS, BUT I HAD PLACED A HORRIBLE CURSE UPON MY OWN HEAD - AS REAL AS ANY CRIME.

WE JOURNEYED ON TO PERTH - BUT I COULD NOT LAUGH OR TALK WITH THE PEOPLE WE MET.
HENRY, I WANT TO MAKE THIS TRIP ALONE.
ENJOY YOUR STAY HERE, AND I'LL RETURN IN A MONTH OR TWO.
LEAVE ME IN PEACE FOR A SHORT WHILE, AND I'LL RETURN A HAPPIER, MORE PLEASANT PERSON.
I'D RATHER STAY WITH YOU THAN BE LEFT HERE WITHOUT YOU.
I'VE MADE MY MIND UP ON THIS.
THEN HURRY BACK --
-- MY DEAR FRIEND.

I FOUND A REMOTE SPOT IN THE NORTHERN HIGHLANDS WHERE I COULD FINISH MY WORK ALONE.
ONLY FIVE PEOPLE LIVED THERE, ALONG WITH A FEW COWS, ON THE BARREN LAND. IT WAS PERFECT!
WHEN I FIRST ARRIVED, I WORKED BY DAY AND SPENT THE EVENINGS WALKING ON THE STONY BEACH.

BUT AS THE DAYS PASSED, I BEGAN TO HATE MY WORK. SOMETIMES, I COULD NOT BRING MYSELF TO ENTER MY LABORATORY...

...AND AT OTHER TIMES, I WORKED DAY AND NIGHT IN A KIND OF FEVER. EVERY MOMENT, I FEARED TO MEET THE MONSTER.

I SUDDENLY THOUGHT ABOUT WHAT I WAS ACTUALLY DOING.

THREE YEARS AGO I HAD CREATED A MONSTER; AND HE HAD DESTROYED LIFE.

I WAS NOW ABOUT TO CREATE YET ANOTHER MONSTER; AND WHO COULD TELL WHAT IT MIGHT DO?

SHE MIGHT BE WORSE THAN THE FIRST MONSTER. SHE MIGHT MURDER FOR PLEASURE.
KRAKK!
KA-BOOM!
HE HAD PROMISED TO LEAVE MANKIND ALONE; BUT SHE HADN'T MADE THAT PROMISE HERSELF...
...SHE MAY REFUSE TO HIDE HERSELF AWAY.

THEY MIGHT EVEN HATE EACH OTHER. WOULD HE FIND HER UGLY?
AND MIGHT SHE TURN AWAY FROM HIM, INCREASING HIS MISERY AS HE WAS DESERTED BY HIS OWN SPECIES AS WELL AS BY ALL MANKIND?
WORSE STILL, THEY MIGHT PRODUCE CHILDREN, STARTING A RACE OF DEVILS TO ROAM THE EARTH. SUCH A RACE WOULD THREATEN THE VERY EXISTENCE OF MAN!
FOR THE FIRST TIME, I REALIZED THE WICKEDNESS OF MY TASK - AND I SHUDDERED AT THE HORROR I MIGHT CREATE.
SUDDENLY...
!?!

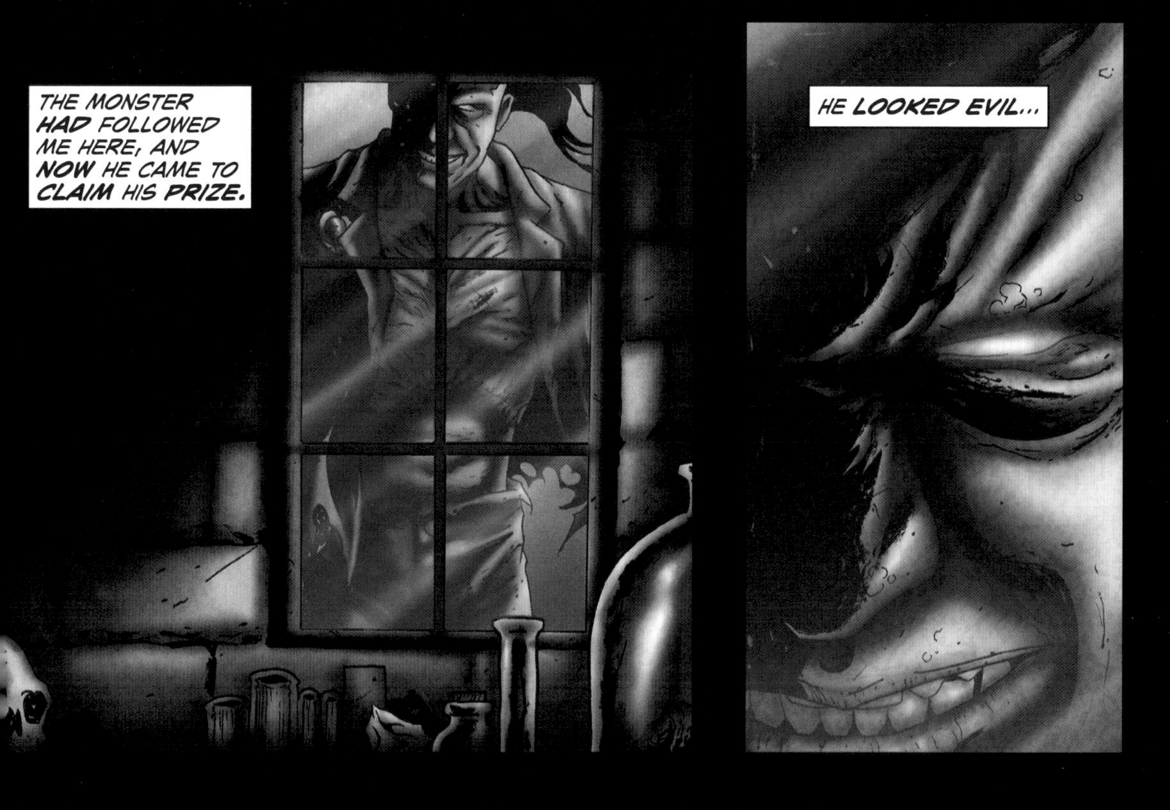
THE MONSTER HAD FOLLOWED ME HERE, AND NOW HE CAME TO CLAIM HIS PRIZE.
HE LOOKED EVIL...

...AND THE THOUGHT OF CREATING ANOTHER LIKE HIM DROVE ME TO MADNESS.

AAAARRRRRGGHHH!
SQUELCH!
THUD!
THUNK!
THE MONSTER WATCHED IN HORROR AS I DESTROYED THE ONLY CREATURE THAT COULD BRING HIM FUTURE HAPPINESS.

WITH A HOWL OF DEVILISH DESPAIR, HE DISAPPEARED.
I VOWED NEVER TO RESUME MY LABORS.
ALONE FOR HOURS, THE SILENCE WAS BROKEN BY THE SOUND OF OARS...
YOU HAVE DESTROYED YOUR WORK! DO YOU INTEND TO BREAK YOUR PROMISE TO ME?
BEGONE!
I WILL NEVER CREATE ANYTHING LIKE YOU AGAIN!
SLAVE, I AM MORE POWERFUL THAN YOU.
YOU ARE MY CREATOR, BUT I AM YOUR MASTER - OBEY!

THREATENING ME ONLY MAKES ME REALIZE THAT I MADE THE RIGHT DECISION.
EACH MAN HAS A MATE, YET I AM ALONE. ARE YOU TO ENJOY HAPPINESS, WHILE I SUFFER IN MISERY?
I SHALL HAVE MY REVENGE!
I GO; BUT REMEMBER, I SHALL BE WITH YOU ON YOUR WEDDING NIGHT.
LUNGE!
VILLAIN!

BEFORE YOU KILL ME, BE SURE OF YOUR OWN SAFETY!
HE DISAPPEARED IN HIS BOAT, AND ALL WAS SILENT AGAIN.
I THOUGHT AGAIN OF HIS WORDS...
"I SHALL BE WITH YOU ON YOUR WEDDING NIGHT."
THAT, THEN, WAS THE DATE SET FOR MY DESTINY. TEARS, THE FIRST I'D CRIED FOR MANY MONTHS, STREAMED FROM MY EYES WHEN I THOUGHT OF ELIZABETH FINDING HER HUSBAND TAKEN FROM HER.
I DECIDED NOT TO GIVE IN WITHOUT A FIGHT.
THE NEXT DAY, I RECEIVED A LETTER FROM CLERVAL ASKING ME TO JOIN HIM. THE LETTER BROUGHT ME BACK TO REALITY.
I FOUND THE COURAGE TO ENTER MY LABORATORY, TO PACK UP MY INSTRUMENTS AND THE REMAINS OF THE HALF-FINISHED CREATURE.
IN THE EARLY MORNING, I SAILED OUT AND CAST THEM INTO THE SEA.
THE QUIET OF THE BOAT ON THE WAVES LULLED ME INTO A PEACEFUL SLEEP...

WHEN I AWOKE, THE SUN WAS HIGH - BUT THE WIND WAS EVEN HIGHER, THREATENING THE SAFETY OF MY LITTLE BOAT.
I TRIED TO CHANGE MY COURSE...
...BUT MY BOAT STARTED TO FILL WITH WATER. MY ONLY HOPE WAS TO GO IN THE DIRECTION OF THE WIND. I HAD NO COMPASS. I WAS UTTERLY LOST.
I THOUGHT THE SEA WAS GOING TO BE MY GRAVE.
MONSTER! YOU'VE FINALLY GOT WHAT YOU WANTED!
HOURS PASSED...
...UNTIL THE WIND CHANGED TO A BREEZE. I WAS SO TIRED, THAT I FELT SICK... ...WHEN SUDDENLY, I SAW LAND.
TEARS GUSHED FROM MY EYES WHEN I KNEW I WAS FINALLY SAFE.

MY GOOD FRIENDS --
-- WHAT IS THIS TOWN CALLED? WHERE AM I?
YOU'LL KNOW SOON ENOUGH.
YOU WON'T HAVE A CHOICE ON WHERE YOU'RE STAYING - I PROMISE YOU THAT.
WHY DO YOU ANSWER SO ROUGHLY?
IT'S NOT LIKE THE ENGLISH TO BE SO NASTY TO STRANGERS.
BUT IT IS THE IRISH CUSTOM TO HATE VILLAINS.
COME WITH ME TO MR. KIRWIN, THE JUDGE.
YOU ARE TO TELL HIM ALL ABOUT THE DEATH OF A MAN WHO WAS MURDERED HERE LAST NIGHT.

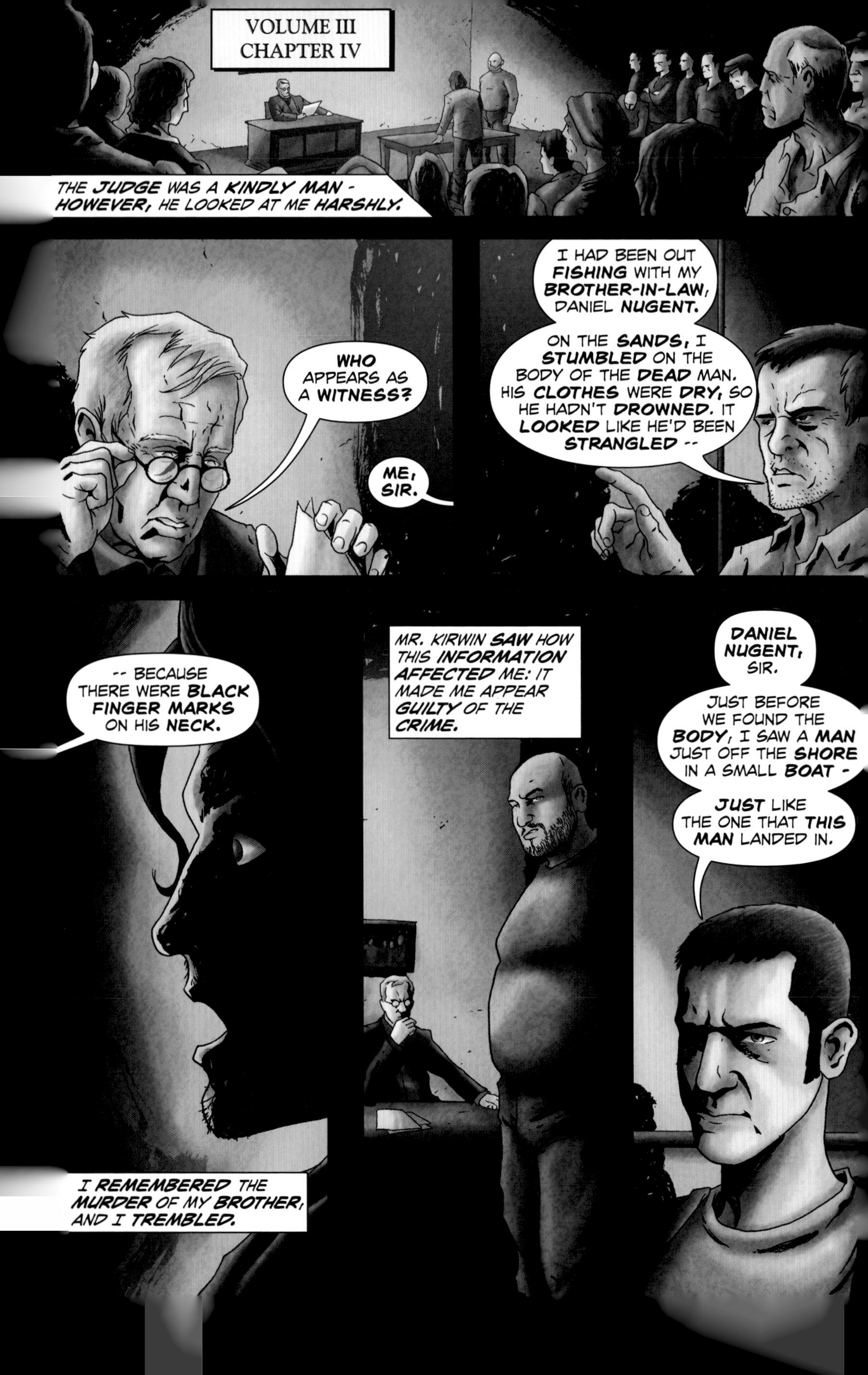
VOLUME III
CHAPTER IV
THE JUDGE WAS A KINDLY MAN - HOWEVER, HE LOOKED AT ME HARSHLY.
WHO APPEARS AS A WITNESS?
ME, SIR.
I HAD BEEN OUT FISHING WITH MY BROTHER-IN-LAW, DANIEL NUGENT.
ON THE SANDS, I STUMBLED ON THE BODY OF THE DEAD MAN. HIS CLOTHES WERE DRY, SO HE HADN'T DROWNED. IT LOOKED LIKE HE'D BEEN STRANGLED --
-- BECAUSE THERE WERE BLACK FINGER MARKS ON HIS NECK.
I REMEMBERED THE MURDER OF MY BROTHER, AND I TREMBLED.
MR. KIRWIN SAW HOW THIS INFORMATION AFFECTED ME: IT MADE ME APPEAR GUILTY OF THE CRIME.
DANIEL NUGENT, SIR.
JUST BEFORE WE FOUND THE BODY, I SAW A MAN JUST OFF THE SHORE IN A SMALL BOAT -
JUST LIKE THE ONE THAT THIS MAN LANDED IN.

A WOMAN ALSO SAW A BOAT WITH A MAN IN IT LEAVE THE SHORE WHERE THE CORPSE WAS FOUND.

THEY ALL AGREED THAT WITH THE STRONG WIND, I'D BEEN DRIVEN BACK TO THE SHORE WHERE I'D LEFT THE BODY.

SHOW HIM THE BODY -

I WANT TO SEE HOW HE REACTS.

I WAS RELAXED...

...BECAUSE I KNEW THAT THE PEOPLE ON THE ISLAND I HAD LEFT COULD PROVE MY INNOCENCE.

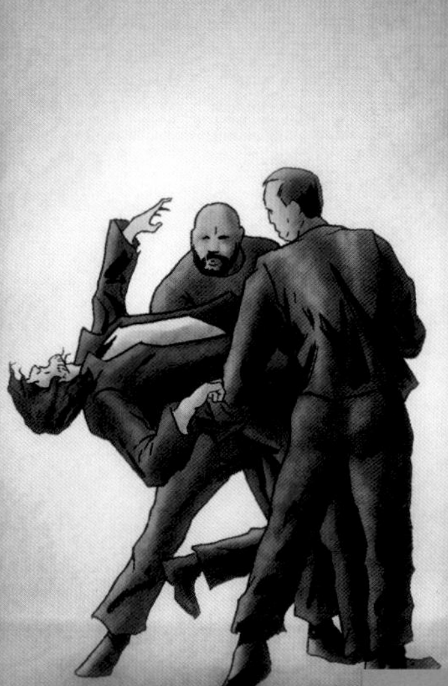

FRIGHTFUL RAVINGS, IN A FITFUL FEVER FOLLOWED FOR TWO MONTHS.
I CALLED MYSELF THE MURDERER OF WILLIAM, JUSTINE AND OF CLERVAL.
FORTUNATELY, ONLY MR. KIRWIN UNDERSTOOD MY NATIVE LANGUAGE - BUT MY CRIES FRIGHTENED THE PEOPLE AROUND ME.
WHY DID I NOT DIE? I WAS MORE MISERABLE THAN ANY MAN HAD BEEN BEFORE.
BUT I WAS DOOMED TO LIVE. AFTER TWO MONTHS, I AWOKE IN PRISON.
ARE YOU BETTER NOW, SIR?
I BELIEVE I AM;
BUT I'M SORRY THAT I'M STILL ALIVE TO FEEL THIS MISERY AND HORROR.

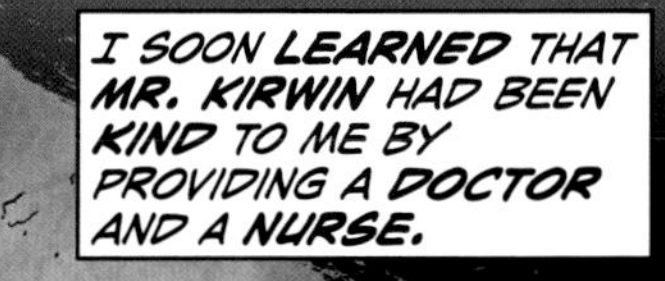

OH NO!!

WHO HAS BEEN KILLED NOW?!?

YOUR FAMILY IS PERFECTLY WELL--

--AND SOMEONE IS HERE TO SEE YOU.
FATHER! YOU'RE SAFE!
AND ELIZABETH?
AND ERNEST?
ALL SAFE.
OH SON -
YOU TRAVELED TO FIND HAPPINESS, BUT FOUND MISERY;
POOR CLERVAL...
I HAD TO TRAVEL NEARLY A HUNDRED MILES TO APPEAR IN THE COUNTY COURT. MR. KIRWIN ARRANGED MY DEFENSE.
THE GRAND JURY FOUND ME INNOCENT.
SOON AFTERWARDS, I WAS RELEASED FROM PRISON - FREE TO BREATHE THE FRESH AIR, AND ABLE TO RETURN TO GENEVA.
BUT FOR ME, WHEREVER I WENT WAS HATEFUL. MY LIFE HAD BEEN POISONED FOREVER.
I THOUGHT ABOUT ENDING MY LIFE - YET ONE DUTY REMAINED: I HAD TO LOOK AFTER THOSE PEOPLE I SO FONDLY LOVED...
...AND I HAD TO LIE IN WAIT FOR THE MURDERER.

VOLUME III
CHAPTER V
WHEN WE REACHED PARIS, I RECEIVED A LETTER FROM ELIZABETH:
...TELL ME, DEAREST VICTOR - DO YOU LOVE ANOTHER?
I CONFESS MY LOVE TO YOU, BUT IT IS YOUR HAPPINESS THAT I DESIRE, AS WELL AS MY OWN.
- ELIZABETH
I REMEMBERED THE THREAT OF THE FIEND - "I SHALL BE WITH YOU ON YOUR WEDDING NIGHT."
ON THAT NIGHT HE HAD DECIDED TO KILL ME. OH, SWEET ELIZABETH - I WOULD DIE TO MAKE HER HAPPY.
MY BELOVED ELIZABETH, I FEAR THAT LITTLE HAPPINESS REMAINS FOR US ON EARTH; YET ALL MY FUTURE HAPPINESS IS CENTERED ON YOU.
I HAVE ONE DREADFUL SECRET WHICH WILL FILL YOU WITH HORROR - AND I WILL CONFESS THIS TO YOU THE DAY AFTER OUR MARRIAGE. UNTIL THEN, YOU MUST NOT MENTION IT.
- VICTOR
WE RETURNED TO GENEVA, WHERE ELIZABETH WELCOMED ME WITH WARM AFFECTION.

ARE YOU ALREADY PROMISED TO SOMEONE ELSE?
NO - I LOVE ELIZABETH AND LOOK FORWARD TO OUR WEDDING.
LET US FIX THE DATE NOW.
WE WERE MARRIED TEN DAYS LATER. I CARRIED PISTOLS AND A DAGGER TO PROTECT ME FROM THE MONSTER.
ELIZABETH SEEMED HAPPY, AND MY FATHER WAS OVERJOYED...
...BUT I HAD ONLY PREPARED FOR MY OWN DEATH; NOT THAT OF ANYONE CLOSE TO ME.

MY FATHER HAD ARRANGED FOR ELIZABETH TO INHERIT A SMALL VILLA ON THE SHORES OF LAKE COMO, WHICH BELONGED TO HER FAMILY. WE PLANNED TO SPEND OUR FIRST DAYS THERE.

WE COMMENCED OUR JOURNEY BY WATER, HEADING TOWARD EVIAN, WHERE WE WOULD STAY THE NIGHT.

VOLUME III
CHAPTER VI
WE TOOK A SHORT WALK ALONG THE SHORE.
A VIOLENT STORM CAME - WATCHFUL AND ANXIOUS, I REACHED FOR MY PISTOL.
WHAT IS IT, VICTOR?
IT'LL BE ALL RIGHT, MY LOVE.
IT'S JUST A BAD STORM.
PLEASE GO TO BED, ELIZABETH - I WILL JOIN YOU LATER.
VICTOR...

I SEARCHED EVERYWHERE FOR THE MONSTER...
...BUT I DISCOVERED NO TRACE OF HIM.
I REALIZED WHAT WAS HAPPENING!
ELIZABETH!!!
I FELL, SENSELESS, TO THE GROUND.

WHEN I RECOVERED, I RUSHED TOWARDS HER AND HELD HER IN MY ARMS.
LIKE HIS OTHER VICTIMS, THE MONSTER HAD STRANGLED MY BELOVED ELIZABETH!
I LOOKED UP AT THE WINDOW...
...TO SEE THE MONSTER SMIRKING AND POINTING TOWARDS THE DEAD BODY OF MY WIFE.
BLAM!

BLAM!
HE GOT AWAY, PLUNGING INTO THE LAKE.
THE SOUND OF THE GUNFIRE ATTRACTED A CROWD, WHO HELPED ME TO LOOK FOR THE FIEND. AFTER SEVERAL HOURS, WE GAVE UP THE SEARCH.
I WAS IN SHOCK.
THE DEATHS OF WILLIAM, JUSTINE, CLERVAL, AND NOW MY WIFE...
...MY FATHER AND ERNEST MIGHT BE NEXT!
I DECIDED TO RETURN IMMEDIATELY TO GENEVA.

MY FATHER AND ERNEST WERE SAFE, BUT THE NEWS OF ELIZABETH'S DEATH WAS HARD FOR MY FATHER TO BEAR.
CURSED BE THE FIEND THAT BROUGHT MISERY ON HIS GREY HAIRS.
IT WAS ALL TOO MUCH FOR HIM, AND IN A FEW DAYS HE DIED IN MY ARMS.
F ME THEN?
NSES, AND WAS
A DARK, SOLITARY
LLED ME MAD.

WHEN I WAS WELL ENOUGH TO BE RELEASED, I VISITED A CRIMINAL JUDGE TO TELL HIM MY STORY.
SIR, I KNOW THE MURDERER,
AND I WANT YOU TO INSTRUCT THE AUTHORITIES TO FIND HIM.
SIR, I'LL DO ALL THAT I CAN.
THANK YOU.
MY TALE MAY BE VERY STRANGE, BUT I CAN ASSURE YOU, IT IS ALL TRUE...
I TOLD MY STORY, GIVING DATES FOR ACCURACY.
IT IS YOUR DUTY, NOW, TO SEIZE AND PUNISH THIS VILLAIN.
I DON'T THINK WE'D EVER BE ABLE TO CATCH THIS CREATURE.
BESIDES - WHO KNOWS WHERE HE MAY BE LIVING NOW.
YOU REFUSE TO HELP ME!
THEN I'LL DO IT MYSELF - I WON'T REST UNTIL HE IS DESTROYED!!

VOLUME III
CHAPTER VII
REVENGE WAS ALL I THOUGHT ABOUT. I DECIDED TO LEAVE GENEVA FOREVER.
I FOUND MYSELF AT THE CEMETERY WHERE MY FAMILY LAY.
ELIZABETH FRANKENSTEIN
I COULD FEEL THE SPIRITS OF MY LOVED ONES AROUND ME.
BY THE SACRED EARTH ON WHICH I KNEEL, AND THE ETERNAL GRIEF THAT I FEEL, I SWEAR TO
PURSUE THE DEMON
WHO CAUSED THIS MISERY UNTIL ONE OR BOTH OF US ARE DEAD!
LET THE CURSED AND HELLISH MONSTER DRINK DEEP OF AGONY;
LET HIM FEEL THE DESPAIR THAT NOW TORMENTS ME!
HA HA HA HA HA!
YOU HAVE DECIDED TO LIVE. MISERABLE WRETCH!
I LUNGED FOR HIM, BUT HE ESCAPED.
I WENT AFTER HIM, AND I HAVE BEEN FOLLOWING HIM EVER SINCE.

I THOUGHT I WAS ABOUT TO SINK, WHEN I SAW YOUR SHIP APPROACHING.

I DREAD DEATH - FOR MY TASK IS UNFINISHED; BUT IF I DIE, WALTON, SWEAR TO ME THAT YOU WILL FIND AND KILL HIM.

LETTER - AUGUST 26TH
MY DEAR MARGARET, YOU HAVE NOW HEARD THIS STRANGE AND HORRIFIC STORY. I DO NOT DOUBT THAT MY FRIEND SPEAKS THE TRUTH. SOMETIMES I ASKED HIM DETAILS ABOUT THE CREATURE'S FORMATION...
ARE YOU MAD? DO YOU WISH TO CREATE SUCH AN EVIL CREATURE YOURSELF?
LEARN FROM MY MISTAKES AND DO NOT ALLOW CURIOSITY TO BE THE SOURCE OF MISERY.
I HAVE FINALLY FOUND THE FRIEND I WAS LOOKING FOR; YET HIS OBSESSION MAKES HIM REFUSE MY FRIENDSHIP.
THANK YOU FOR YOUR KINDNESS, WALTON; BUT ALL MY FRIENDS ARE DEAD, AND THEY CANNOT BE REPLACED.
ONLY ONE THOUGHT KEEPS ME ALIVE - I MUST PURSUE AND DESTROY THE MONSTER THAT I CREATED.
THEN MY WORK WILL BE DONE, AND I MAY DIE.
LETTER - SEPTEMBER 2ND
THE LIVES OF THESE BRAVE MEN ARE AT RISK - AND THEY LOOK TO ME FOR LEADERSHIP. THEY ARE MY RESPONSIBILITY.

LETTER - SEPTEMBER 5TH
I THOUGHT THAT THE MEN WERE UNEASY - I WAS WORRIED ABOUT A MUTINY.
CAPTAIN, WE INSIST THAT ONCE THE SHIP IS FREED, WE HEAD TO THE SOUTH.
YOU CANNOT REFUSE.
YOU DEMAND OF YOUR CAPTAIN?
ARE YOU RUNNING AWAY AT THE FIRST SIGN OF DANGER?
THIS WAS TO BE A GLORIOUS EXPEDITION. YOU CANNOT RETURN TO YOUR FAMILIES IN DISGRACE. RETURN AS HEROES, WHO HAVE FOUGHT AND WON - AND WHO HAVE NOT TURNED THEIR BACK ON THE ENEMY.
THE MEN WERE UNABLE TO REPLY.
GIVE THIS SOME THOUGHT.
I WILL NOT LEAD YOU FARTHER NORTH UNLESS YOU AGREE TO IT.
AYE, CAPTAIN.

September 12th.

I am returning to England.
I have lost my hopes of glory - and I have lost my friend.

Three days ago, the ice began to move. By this time, my unfortunate guest was entirely confined to his bed.

I WILL NOT COME WITH YOU.
YOU MAY GIVE UP YOUR PURPOSE, BUT MINE REMAINS.
I AM WEAK, BUT THE SPIRITS WHO HELP ME SHALL GIVE ME STRENGTH...
HE MADE AN ATTEMPT TO GET OUT OF HIS BED - BUT HE FELL BACK, EXHAUSTED.
THE SURGEON TOLD ME THAT HE ONLY HAD A FEW HOURS TO LIVE.
Alas! My strength is gone. I feel that I shall soon die, while my enemy still lives.
In a fit of madness, I made a rational creature. He destroyed my family and friends - and, miserable himself, he ought to die.
Yet I cannot ask you to sacrifice all for this task.

I must go now to the arms of the beloved dead.
Farewell, Walton!
Seek happiness in peace...
Shelley Poems

HE SQUEEZED MY HAND AND CLOSED HIS EYES... ...FOREVER.
MARGARET, WHAT CAN I SAY ABOUT THE DEATH OF THIS WONDERFUL MAN?
CLUMP
THAT NOISE...
...A VOICE...
...FROM FRANKENSTEIN'S CABIN!
GREAT GOD!
WHEN HE HEARD ME, HE SPRUNG TO THE WINDOW.
STAY!

THAT IS ALSO MY VICTIM! HIS IS MY LAST MURDER!
OH FRANKENSTEIN - CAN YOU EVER FORGIVE ME? I WHO DESTROYED YOU BY DESTROYING ALL YOU LOVED?
ALAS - HE CANNOT ANSWER ME.
MY DUTY TO CARRY OUT FRANKENSTEIN'S DYING WISH WAS HALTED BY MY CURIOSITY.
IF YOU HAD TOLD HIM YOUR REGRET A TIME AGO, HE WOULD STILL BE ALIVE TODAY.
DO YOU THINK THAT I DIDN'T FEEL PAINFUL REGRET?
I SUFFERED MORE THAN HE DID IN MY OWN CREATION.
THE GROANS OF MY VICTIMS WERE MORE TORTURE THAN YOU CAN EVER IMAGINE.
I PITIED HIM - BUT WHEN I DISCOVERED THAT HE HOPED FOR HAPPINESS, THEN I WAS FILLED WITH A THIRST FOR VENGEANCE.
I WAS A SLAVE TO MY EVIL WAYS, AND IT MADE ME MISERABLE --
-- EXCEPT WHEN SHE DIED - THEN, EVIL BECAME MY GOOD!
AND NOW IT IS ENDED - THERE IS MY LAST VICTIM!
WRETCH! HOW CAN YOU COMPLAIN ABOUT THE MISERY YOU HAVE CAUSED?
YOUR REGRET IS BECAUSE THE TARGET OF YOUR EVIL IS NO LONGER WITHIN YOUR POWER.
NO - IT IS NOT THAT WAY.

I DO NOT LOOK FOR SYMPATHY. I AM CONTENT TO SUFFER ALONE.
ONCE I HOPED FOR HUMAN FRIENDSHIP, BUT NOW CRIME HAS PUT ME BENEATH THE LOWEST CREATURE.
NO GUILT OR MISERY CAN BE FOUND THAT COMPARES TO MINE.
WHEN I REMEMBER ALL THAT I HAVE DONE, I CANNOT BELIEVE THAT I AM THE SAME CREATURE THAT ONCE WANTED ONLY GOODNESS.
THE FALLEN ANGEL HAS BECOME A TERRIBLE, SOLITARY, DEVIL.

YOU SEEM TO KNOW ALL ABOUT ME --
-- BUT FRANKENSTEIN COULD NOT TELL YOU ABOUT THE MONTHS OF MISERY THAT I ENDURED.
AM I THE ONLY CRIMINAL HERE, WHEN ALL MANKIND HAS SINNED AGAINST ME?
BUT IT IS TRUE THAT I AM A MURDERER.
I HAVE CAUSED GREAT MISERY FOR MY CREATOR, WHO LIES THERE - COLD AND WHITE IN DEATH.
YOU HATE ME --
-- YET I HATE MYSELF EVEN MORE THAN YOU EVER CAN.
I WON'T CAUSE ANY FURTHER HARM.
MY WORK IS NEARLY COMPLETE. ONLY MY *OWN* DEATH REMAINS.

I SHALL HEAD NORTH AND CONSUME MY BODY WITH FLAMES - REDUCING IT TO ASHES SO THAT NO OTHER SUCH WRETCH AS I MAY BE CREATED.
I SHALL DIE.
I SHALL NO LONGER FEEL THE AGONY OF EXISTENCE.
MY CREATOR IS DEAD - AND WHEN I AM NO MORE, ALL MEMORY OF US BOTH WILL BE GONE.
I SHALL NO LONGER SEE THE SUN OR STARS, OR FEEL THE BREEZE ON MY CHEEKS; ALL WILL PASS AWAY, AND IN THIS STATE I MUST FIND MY HAPPINESS.

SOON I SHALL DIE - AND THESE BURNING MISERIES WILL END. I SHALL REJOICE IN THE AGONY OF THE TORTURING FLAMES!
AAAARRRRGGGHHH!!!...

THE LIGHT OF THE FIRE WILL FADE AWAY, AND MY ASHES SHALL BE SCATTERED BY THE WINDS...
...AND MY SPIRIT WILL SLEEP IN PEACE.

FAREWELL! YOU SHALL BE THE LAST HUMAN I SHALL SEE.
FAREWELL, FRANKENSTEIN! AS MISERABLE AS YOU WERE --
-- MY AGONY WAS STILL GREATER THAN YOURS!
THUDD!!!
HE WAS SOON FAR AWAY - LOST IN THE DARKNESS AND DISTANCE.

MARGARET, WHAT CAN I SAY THAT WOULD MAKE YOU UNDERSTAND? NO WORDS CAN EXPLAIN.

BUT I RETURN TO ENGLAND, AND THERE I MAY FIND CONSOLATION.

Frankenstein
End

Mary Shelley

1797-1851

"It is not singular that, as the daughter of two persons of distinguished literary celebrity, I should very early in life have thought of writing."

National Portrait Gallery, London

Mary Shelley was born Mary Wollstonecraft Godwin in Somers Town, London in August 1797. Her father, William Godwin, was a famous philosopher, novelist and journalist. Her mother was Mary Wollstonecraft, who was a feminist philosopher, educator, and writer, well known for her work ***A Vindication of the Rights of Woman*** (1792). In it, she argued that women were not naturally inferior to men, but they appeared that way due to a lack of education (education did not become compulsory in England until the Education Act of 1870). She suggested that both men and women should be treated equally, and as rational beings in a society that operated upon reason and logic.

Despite William and Mary's revolutionary attitudes to the social order of the time, and the fact that Mary already had a daughter, Fanny Imlay, from a previous relationship, they married in March 1797 to ensure the legitimacy of their coming child.

Sadly, Mary Wollstonecraft died of puerperal fever (sometimes called "childbed fever") a few days after giving birth, leaving William Godwin alone to bring up baby Mary and her older half-sister Fanny. He believed himself **"totally unfitted to educate them"** and felt that a substitute mother should be found. He didn't look far! William Godwin married his next-door neighbor, Mary Jane Vial (better known as Mary Jane Clairmont) on December 21, 1801. Mary Jane brought two children of her own into the marriage: Charles and Jane (who later called herself Claire). Then, in 1803, Mary Jane gave birth to William Godwin Junior - bringing the total to five children living under the same roof.

Mary Wollstonecraft Godwin did not have a "formal" education, but was taught to read and write at home. Her father encouraged her to write from an early age. She was given freedom to access his extensive library and allowed to listen to the political, philosophical, scientific and literary discussions that he conducted with his friends —William Wordsworth and Samuel Taylor Coleridge were among the many distinguished visitors to the house at this time.

William and Jane Godwin started a publishing company in 1805 (M. Godwin and Co.) and opened a shop selling children's books. The couple also wrote children's books themselves, often under the name of Edward Baldwin.

In 1810, they published what was possibly Mary's first work: ***Mounseer Nongtongpaw; or the Discoveries of John Bull on a Trip to Paris,*** a verse poem. It is hard to say whether this was in fact Mary's first work, as all of her early papers were lost, and nothing of her surviving writing can be dated prior to 1814 with any certainty.

In 1812, possibly due to growing conflict with her stepmother, Mary went to live for several months in Dundee with the family of William Baxter, who was a friend of her father's.

Around the same time, the famous poet Percy Bysshe Shelley (a devoted follower, friend and sponsor of Mary's father) began spending a great deal of time in the Godwin home. Percy, along with his young wife Harriet and sister-in-law Eliza, would regularly dine there; and Mary would have met Percy on her return visits to London. By then, aged nineteen, Shelley had already been expelled from Oxford University and his family would only talk to him through lawyers.

Percy and Mary began to meet outside of her home, often at the grave of Mary's mother in St. Pancras Churchyard, where Mary used to sit and read her mother's works. Their relationship developed quickly - much to the horror of Mary's father, who forbade the lovers to meet.

Disregarding the views of her father and of society as a whole, on July 18, 1814, when Mary was only sixteen years old, the lovers ran away to France, taking Jane Clairmont (Mary's stepsister, who later called herself Claire) with them. Mary also took a box containing her writings and letters; and unfortunately, this precious box was lost during the journey.

After only two months, the travelers returned to London. They were penniless, and Shelley was forced to hide from people he owed money to. Mary's father still strongly disapproved of the relationship and would not even meet with his daughter or her lover. Mary, unmarried and barely seventeen, was now pregnant. To make matters worse, Percy Shelley's wife, Harriet, was also pregnant. Harriet gave birth to a son in 1814 and sued her husband for custody of their children and for financial support - leaving Percy in terrible financial difficulty.

From her sparse journal entries of this time, it would appear that the young couple still enjoyed a reasonable standard of living and had a close circle of friends – which was surprising as their behavior would have been considered scandalous by the "respectable" society of the day.

Percy Shelley's grandfather, Sir Bysshe Shelley, died in January 1815. This left Percy as "heir apparent" to the title and to the family estate on the death of his father. It also greatly improved the Shelleys' financial situation; and by June 1815, Percy was in receipt of an annual allowance of £1,000 – a huge amount of money at a time when the average annual wage for a weaver was only £16 (seventy-two pennies per week).

However, the relationship between Mary and Percy was sadly to be put under further strain. Their first daughter was born two months premature and died within a few days. This was to have a lasting effect on Mary, as she wrote in her journal on March 19, 1815:

> **"Dream that my little baby came to life again – that it had only been cold & that we rubbed it by the fire & it lived – I awake & find no baby – I think about the little thing all day – not in good spirits – Shelley is very unwell."**

Almost immediately, Mary became pregnant again and a second, healthy child, William, was born a year later. During this time, Shelley's health was deteriorating (possibly through a weak heart) and the continuing but not always welcome presence of Mary's stepsister - now known as Claire - can only have added further pressure to the couple's relationship.

The following year of 1816 was no less eventful. Claire had become pregnant by the poet Lord George Byron. She needed to establish with Byron that the child was indeed his, and so persuaded Percy and Mary to accompany her to Switzerland to meet him at Lake Geneva. By June, they had settled near Cologny - and it was here that Mary began to write *Frankenstein*; she was still only eighteen. In her original preface to the book, she wrote:

> **"I passed the summer of 1816 in the environs of Geneva. The season was cold and rainy, and in the evenings we crowded around a blazing wood fire, and occasionally amused ourselves with some German stories of ghosts, which happened to fall into our hands. These tales excited in us a playful desire of imitation. Two other friends (a tale from the pen of one of whom would be far more acceptable to the public than any thing I can ever hope to produce) and myself agreed to write each a story founded on some supernatural occurrence."**

They returned to London in September 1816. In October, Mary's older half-sister Fanny committed suicide through a laudanum overdose. In November, Percy Shelley's pregnant wife Harriet went missing and was eventually found drowned in the River Serpentine. She was just twenty-one years old - and her death greatly added to the scandal that already dogged the couple. Amidst all of this drama, Mary Wollstonecraft married Percy Shelley on December 30, 1816 at St. Mildred's Church in London.

Frankenstein was eventually completed in May 1817, but wasn't published until 1818 – and even then, Mary wasn't named as the author (*Frankenstein* wasn't published in her name until 1831).

In September 1817, Mary gave birth to her third child, Clara Everina. Percy owed money once again, and the family, along with Claire and her young child, moved across Europe to the warmer climes of Italy.

Tragically, Clara Everina died in Venice in 1818; and in the following year, their son William died of Malaria in Rome. These losses had a profound effect on Mary, who sank into a deep depression. Percy wrote in his notebook:

"My dearest Mary, wherefore hast thou gone,
And left me in this dreary world alone?
Thy form is here indeed—a lovely one—
But thou art fled, gone down a dreary road
That leads to Sorrow's most obscure abode.
For thine own sake I cannot follow thee
Do thou return for mine."

The Shelleys moved to Florence in October 1819, where their son Percy Florence was born the following month. His birth lifted Mary's spirits and brought the couple closer together again.

In May 1822, they moved on to La Spezia, where Mary miscarried on June 16, during her fifth pregnancy. Percy insisted that she should sit in a bath of ice until the doctor arrived – and that advice saved her life.

Percy Shelley was not a strong swimmer, and some say that he couldn't swim at all; yet despite that, and even though he had once nearly drowned in a boating accident, he and several friends decided to spend the summer of 1822 sailing on the Bay of Lerici. On July 18, the drowned bodies of Percy, his friend Edward Williams and a young sailor by the name of Charles Vivian were washed ashore. In keeping with the quarantine regulations of the time, Percy Shelley's body was cremated on the beach near Viareggio. His heart was snatched from the funeral pyre by Edward Trelawny - adventurer, author and friend of the poets – who had designed the boat that sank.

In 1823, Shelley's ashes were interred in a burial plot in the Cimitero Acattolico in Rome, under an ancient pyramid in the city walls. The Latin inscription reads, **"Cor Cordium"**, which translates to **"Heart of Hearts"**. It also bears a few lines from Shakespeare's ***The Tempest***:

"Nothing of him that doth fade
But doth suffer a sea change
into something rich & strange"

Back in England, ***The Courier*** (a leading newspaper of the time) published a notice of the death of Shelley:-

"Shelley, the writer of some infidel poetry has been drowned; now he knows whether there is a God or no."

Mary and her only surviving child, Percy Florence, left Italy in the summer of 1823 and returned to England.

Percy Shelley's allowance ended when he died. His father, Sir Timothy Shelley, provided Mary and his grandson with only a very small sum of money – and even that was on the condition that she did not publish any of his son's remaining manuscripts and that she did not write under her married name. It is to satisfy this last condition that all of her publications avoid the use of an author's name, and instead say, "By the Author of ***Frankenstein***."

In 1824 she wrote in her journal:

"At the age of twenty six I am in the condition of an aged person--all my old friends are gone ... & my heart fails when I think by how few ties I hold to the world...."

She did not remarry; in fact she turned down more than one proposal, saying that after being married to one genius, she could only marry another. She concentrated on earning money from her writing, while looking after her father, William, until his death in 1836. Percy Florence followed in his father's footsteps, going to public school and on to university. He inherited his grandfather's baronetcy in 1844, becoming Sir Percy Florence Shelley, 3rd Baronet.

Although Mary continued to write, none of her later works are as well known or as powerful as her first novel, ***Frankenstein*** (she died before completing the biography of her husband). From 1839 onwards, she suffered from several illnesses, including headaches and bouts of paralysis, which at times prevented her from writing; and she was blighted by ill health in her final years. In 1848, Percy Florence married Jane Gibson St. John. Mary divided her time between living with them at their country home in Sussex and at her own home in Chester Square, London.

Mary Wollstonecraft Shelley died on February 1, 1851 aged fifty-three. The cause of death is recorded as **"Disease of the brain – supposed tumour in left hemisphere of long standing"**. She is buried next to her parents at St. Peter's Church in Bournemouth, on the southern English coast.

After her death, Mary's box desk was opened. In it were locks of her dead children's hair, a notebook she had shared with Percy Bysshe Shelley, and a copy of his poem *Adonaïs*, with one page folded around a silk parcel containing some of his ashes and the remains of his heart.

Mary Shelley's Family Tree

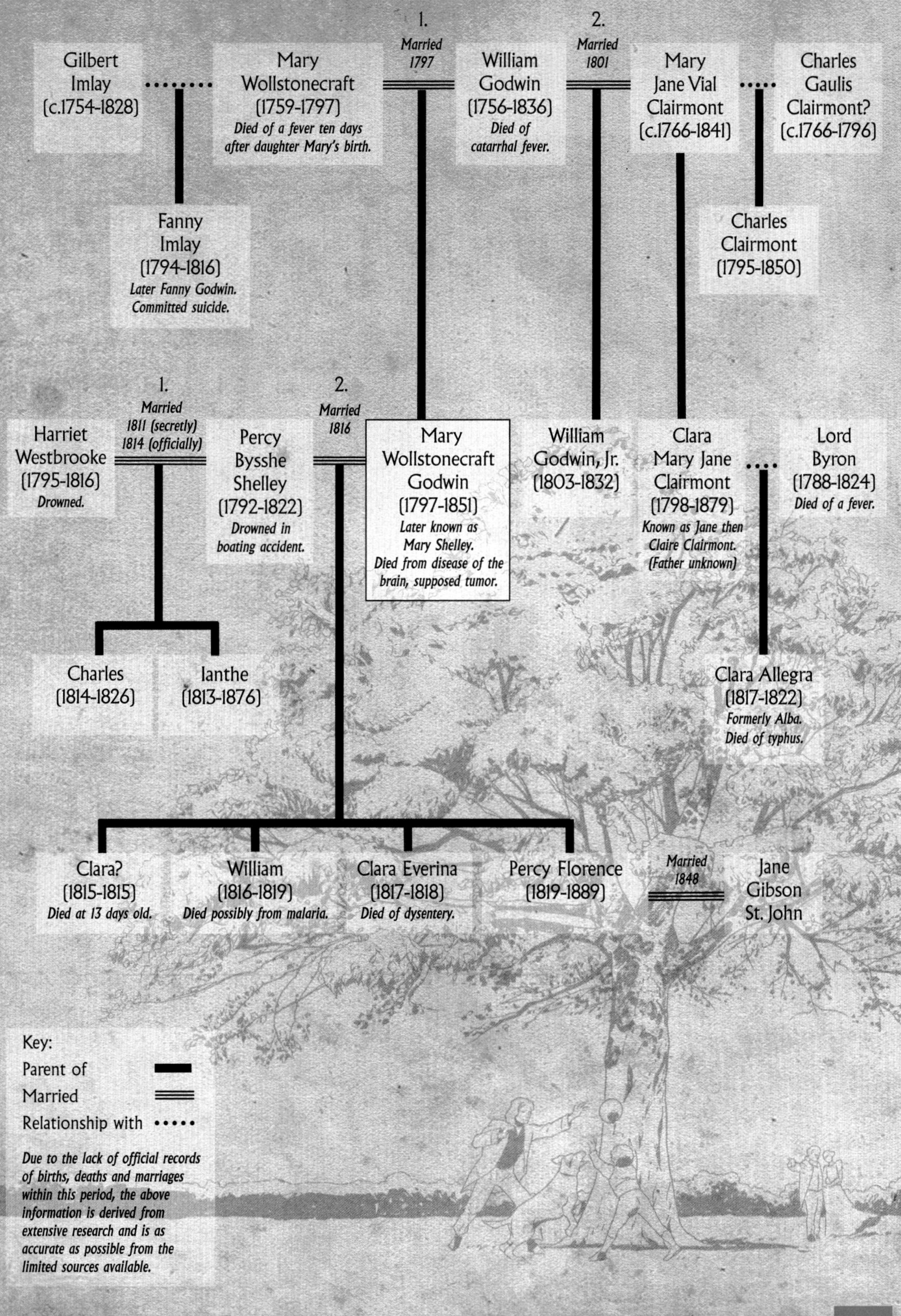

1816...The Birth of Frankenstein

"How I, then a young girl, came to think of, and to dilate upon, so very hideous an idea?"

The year of 1816 saw crop failure and famine, food riots across Europe following the end of the Napoleonic wars, and a heavy June snow fall in New England. France sentenced Napoleon Bonaparte to permanent exile in St. Helena, and the author of *Jane Eyre*, Charlotte Brontë, was born in England.

Eighteen-year-old Mary Wollstonecraft Godwin spent the summer of 1816 with her poet lover Percy Bysshe Shelley and her stepsister Claire Clairmont at Maison Chapuis near Colgny in Geneva, Switzerland. They were there to visit Lord Byron and confirm that he was indeed the father of Claire's unborn child.

The weather was peculiar in 1816 – in fact it became known as "the year without a summer", or "The Poverty Year". Temperatures fluctuated between beautiful summer days and near freezing temperatures within a matter of hours. These unusual conditions were most likely the result of the eruption of Volcano Tambora in Indonesia. In addition to temperature variations, torrential rains and terrifying lightning storms plagued the area, with sunsets being particularly spectacular due to the vast quantities of ash in the air. It was this abnormal weather, coupled with the mood of the group and the wilder aspects of the Swiss landscape, that contributed to the birth of the story of *Frankenstein*.

Chapter 7th 21 / 45

It was on a dreary night of November
that I beheld my man compleated and
with an anxiety that almost amount
ed to agony I collected instruments of life
around me that I might infuse a
spark of being into the lifeless thing
that lay at my feet. It was already
one in the morning, the rain pattered
dismally against the window panes &
my candle was nearly burnt out, when
by the glimmer of the half extinguish
ed light I saw the dull yellow eye of
the creature open. It breathed hard,
and a convulsive motion agitated
its limbs.

How can I describe my
emotion at this catastrophe, or how deli
neate the wretch whom with such
infinite pains and care I had endeavoured
to form. His limbs were in proportion
and I had selected his features as
beautiful. Beautiful! Great God! His
yellow skin scarcely covered the work of
muscles and arteries beneath; his hair
was of a lustrous black & flowing and his teeth of a pearly white
ness but these luxuriances only
formed a more horrid contrast with
his watery eyes that seemed almost of
the same colour as the dun white
sockets in which they were set,

Due to a particularly violent storm on the night of June 16, 1816, Mary and Percy could not return to Maison Chapuis, and so were invited to spend the night with Lord Byron and John Polidori, Byron's young physician, at Villa Diodati. The group read aloud from *The Fantasmagoriana*, a collection of ghost stories translated from German into French, that they had found in the villa. In one of the stories, a group of travelers entertain each other with tales of supernatural experiences; and this inspired Byron to challenge the group to each write a ghost story.

Shelley wrote an unrecorded story based on his life experiences; Byron wrote only a fragment of a novel; and Polidori is thought to have begun *The Vampyre* at this time (many consider the main character in this story, Lord Ruthven, to be based on Lord Byron). Mary was lost for ideas that evening; but she continued, days after the challenge had finished, determined to produce a suitable story.

In her own words:

> **"I busied myself to think of a story, – a story to rival those which had excited us to this task. One which would speak to the mysterious fears of our nature, and awaken thrilling horror – one to make the reader dread to look round, to curdle the blood, and quicken the beatings of the heart. If I did not accomplish these things, my ghost story would be unworthy of its name. I thought and pondered – vainly. I felt that blank incapability of invention which is the greatest misery of authorship."**

Below: Two leafs from the first of the two disbound draft notebooks, started by Mary Godwin at Geneva in summer 1816, with marginal corrections by Percy Bysshe Shelley.

The one on the left is where the story actually started: **"It was on a dreary night of November that I beheld my man completed..."** which in the finished book is the first line of Volume I Chapter V.

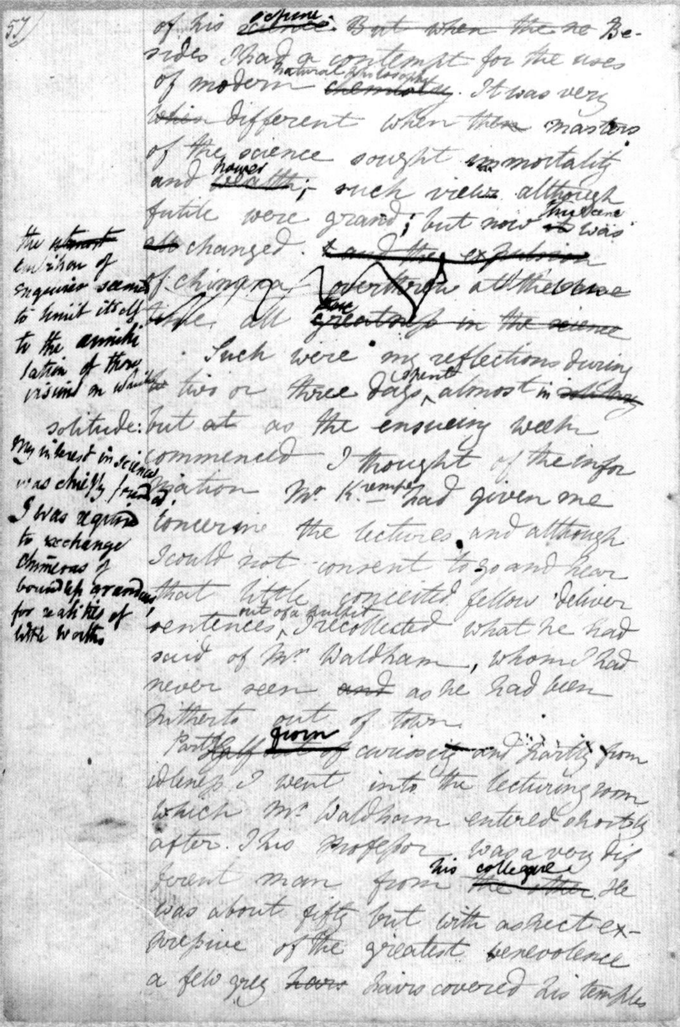

In the days that followed, Mary remained unable to begin her story:

> **"Have you thought of a story? I was asked each morning, and each morning I was forced to reply with a mortifying negative."**

During one gathering of the group that summer, they debated the nature of the principle of life and discussed whether there was any probability of it ever being discovered and communicated. These conversations had a profound effect on Mary. She later wrote that when she went to her bedroom, she had a vision:

> **"I saw the pale student of unhallowed arts kneeling beside the thing he had put together. I saw the hideous phantasm of a man stretched out, then, on the working of some powerful engine, show signs of life...His success would terrify the artist; he would rush away...hope that...this thing...would subside into dead matter...he opens his eyes; behold the horrid thing stands at his bedside, opening his curtains..."**

Mary had at last found her story, and the monster had his creator.

As you can see from the page opposite, she began by writing the lines that open Volume I Chapter V.:

> **"It was on a dreary night of November."**

...and just as in the story, a monster was born!

"(Frankenstein) is the most wonderful work to have been written at twenty years of age that I ever heard of. You are now five and twenty. And, most fortunately, you have pursued a course of reading, and cultivated your mind in a manner the most admirably adapted to make you a great successful author. If you cannot be independent, who should be?"

– William Godwin to Mary Shelley

Frankenstein Lives!

It is testimony to the dramatic nature of the book and the way that it captured the imaginations of people at the time, that a stage version of *Frankenstein* appeared within five years of its first publication.

On 28th July 1823, *Presumption; or The Fate of Frankenstein*, a play with songs by Richard Brinsley Peake, opened at the English Opera House, and ran for thirty-seven performances. The monster was played by T.P. Cooke; and according to one account, his make-up left him with a

> "shrivelled complexion, lips straight and black, and a horrible ghastly grin."

The monster is mute in this first adaptation. This has also been the case in many adaptations since, despite Mary Shelley's creation being tormented, tragic and well-spoken.

An 1823 poster from the English Opera House production of the play entitled *Presumption; or, The Fate of Frankenstein*

Mary Shelley went to see the production on August 28, 1823 and was mostly complementary about it in her letter to her friend Leigh Hunt on September 9. She writes:

> "*Frankenstein* had prodigious success as a drama & was about to be repeated for the 23rd night at the English Opera House. The play bill amused me extremely, for in the list of dramatis personæ came, ——— by Mr. T. Cooke: this nameless mode of naming the un {n}ameable is rather good. On Friday Aug. 29th, Jane, my father William & I went to the theatre to see it. Wallack looked very well as F—he is at the beginning full of hope & expectation—at the end of the 1st Act. The stage represents a room with a staircase leading to F's workshop—he goes to it and you see his light at a small window, through which a frightened servant peeps, who runs off in terror when F. exclaims "It lives!"—Presently F himself rushes in horror & trepidation from the room and while still expressing his agony & terror ——— throws down the door of the laboratory, leaps the staircase & presents his unearthly & monstrous person on the stage.
> The story is not well managed—but Cooke played ——'s part extremely well—his seeking as it were for support—his trying to grasp at the sounds he heard—all indeed he does was well imagined & executed. I was much amused, & it appeared to excite a breathless eagerness in the audience."

It was well received by the critics, too. This review of the play appeared in a London newspaper the day after the premiere:

> *THEATRE, English Opera*
> *London Morning Post:*
> *Tuesday, July 29 & Wednesday, July 30*
> *Review of Presumption; or the*
> *Fate of Frankenstein (1823)*
>
> "A new three act piece, described as 'a romance of a peculiar interest,' was last night produced at this theatre, entitled, *Presumption, or the Fate of Frankenstein.*
>
> The fable represents Frankenstein, a man of great science, to have succeeded in uniting the remains of dead persons, so as to form one being, which he endows with life. He has, however, little reason to exult in the triumph of his art; for the creature thus formed, hideous in aspect, and possessed of prodigious strength, spreads terror, and carries ruin wherever he goes. Though wearing the human form, he is incapable of associating with mankind, to whom he eventually becomes hostile, and having killed the mistress and brother of Frankenstein, he finally vanquishes his mortal creator, and perishes himself beneath a falling avalanche. Such is the outline of the business of a drama more extraordinary in its plan, than remarkable for strength in its execution. There is something in the piecemeal resurrection effected by Frankenstein, which, instead of creating that awful interest intended to arise from it, gives birth to a feeling of horror. We have not that taste for the monstrous which can enable us to enjoy it in the midst of the most startling absurdities. To Lord BYRON, the late Mr. SHELLEY, and philosophers of that stamp, it might appear a very fine thing to attack the Christian faith from a masked battery, and burlesque the resurrection of the dead, by representing the fragments of departed mortals as starting into existence at the command of a man; but we would prefer the comparatively noble assaults of VOLNEY, VOLTAIRE, and PAINE.
>
> In the first scene in which —— (so the creature of Frankenstein is indicated in the bills) makes his appearance, the effect is terrific. There are other parts in which a very powerful impression is produced on the spectators, but to have made the most of the idea a greater interest ought early in the drama to have been excited for Frankenstein and the destined victims of the non-descript, and he himself would have been an object of greater attention if speech had been vouchsafed. The efforts to relieve the serious action of the Piece by mirth and music were generally successful, and the labours of Mr. WATSON the composer we often loudly applauded.
>
> The acting was very grand. WALLACK as Frankenstein, displayed great feeling and animation; T.P. COOKE as —— (or the made up man), was tremendously appalling. The other performers did as much as could be expected in the parts allotted to them, and the piece though it met with some opposition at the close had a large majority in its favour, and was announced for repetition."

Further dramatizations followed in quick succession. On August 18, 1823 *Frankenstein; or, the Demon of Switzerland*, a play by Henry M. Milner, took to the stage at the Royal Coburg Theatre in London. Three other stage versions followed that same year: *Humgumption; or, Dr. Frankenstein and the Hobgoblin of Hoxton*, *Presumption and the Blue Demon* and *Another Piece of Presumption*, the second play by Peake based on the *Frankenstein* story.

In December 1824, *Frank-in-Steam; or, The Modern Promise to Pay* premiered at the Olympic Theatre; while July 1826 saw the opening at the Royal Coburg Theatre of *The Man and The Monster; or The Fate of Frankenstein*, a further interpretation by Henry M. Milner.

Twenty-three years later in December 1849, *Frankenstein; or, The Model Man*, by William and Robert Brough, opened at the Adelphi Theatre and ran for twenty-six performances.

Interestingly, it is within these early plays that the man and the monster were becoming interchangeable, with writers using *Frankenstein* to describe both the scientist and his creation.

The list of adaptations doesn't end there. Steven Earl Forry, author of *Hideous Progenies: Dramatizations of Frankenstein from Mary Shelley to the Present* and an authority on this dramatic history, has cataloged almost one hundred dramatic adaptations of *Frankenstein* between 1821 and 1986.

Frankenstein on Film

The birth of motion pictures opened up further opportunities to present the story visually. The first cinematic version of *Frankenstein* appeared in 1910. It was a one-reel silent film produced by Edison Films of New York. Their catalogue of the time proudly proclaimed:

> **"we have carefully omitted anything in Mrs. Shelley's story which might shock any portion of the audience."**

This film was assumed to be lost but amazingly was re-discovered in the 1970s, still in a viewable condition. The second *Frankenstein* film was produced in 1915, titled *Life Without Soul* and directed by Joseph W Smiley. The story is of a doctor who creates a man without a soul. At the end of the film, we find out that the young hero has only dreamed the events of the film, after falling asleep reading Mary Shelley's novel. This film is thought to have been lost.

In 1930, Universal Studios bought the film rights to Peggy Webling's play *Frankenstein: An Adventure in the Macabre*, which had premiered in London in 1927. Bela Lugosi was originally put forward as the actor to play the part of the monster. However, a then obscure English actor, William Henry Pratt, who went by the stage name of Boris Karloff, finally got the part. Karloff's success in *Frankenstein* made him an international star, and the film itself became an instant classic of a new genre - the horror movie.

The Granger Collection, New York. Poster for the 1931 film, *Frankenstein* starring Boris Karloff as the monster.

This lumbering and (again) mute creature has perhaps been the most recognizable image of Frankenstein's "monster" since then. The creature's now-famous flat head and neck-bolt make-up was created by Universal Studios' make-up artist Jack P. Pierce.

Frankenstein earned rave reviews and was voted one of the films of the year by the New York Times. It made huge amounts of money; the production cost of around $270,000 was dwarfed by the earnings of more than $12 million.

In all, over fifty films have been made of the *Frankenstein* story, ranging from horror to drama to comedy, such as the brilliant Mel Brooks' *Young Frankenstein* (1974) starring Gene Wilder and Marty Feldman. Unsurprisingly, interest in the story remains as strong as ever today.

2004 saw the release of a TV film based on the *Frankenstein* trilogy of books by Dean R. Koontz. The story takes place in present day New Orleans, where two detectives are hunting the perpetrator of a series of murders. They are assisted by a mysterious "man", who is in fact the first "creation" of a scientist from many years past, and who has been roaming the earth for hundreds of years, searching for his creator and nemesis. The premise of the film is that Mary Shelley based her own book on the story of this "creation".

In contrast, Hallmark Entertainment's four-part TV mini-series, also released in 2004, has often been cited as the most faithful cinematic telling of Mary Shelley's story to date. This adaptation focuses not only on the action, but also on the development of the characters as the story unfolds. It contains all of the important scenes from the novel - including the narratives by Robert Walton – but has one major deviation from the novel: Victor Frankenstein is seen to use electricity from a thunderstorm to give life to his creature. Although this dramatic cinematic effect has been used by the majority of directors over the years, it doesn't appear in Mary Shelley's book.

It is incredible that a story written nearly two hundred years ago should still be part of our everyday culture. Although the popularity of the films has helped, it is mainly the strength of the original story, dealing as it does with complex themes and issues, that has enabled it to survive through the years; from stage to screen, radio to television; and even now being transformed into this full-color graphic novel.

Page Creation

1. Script

In order to create two versions of the same book, the story is first adapted into two scripts: Original Text and Quick Text. While the degree of complexity changes for each script, the artwork remains the same for both books.

Panel 1
In the foreground, the man has the girl now in his arms. She has slightly revived, her own arms wrapped around his neck. This should suggest that he is her father. He is running with her away from the MONSTER, who is pursuing them into the wood.

	ORIGINAL TEXT	QUICK TEXT
CAPTION MONSTER V/O	Tearing the girl from my arms, he hastened towards the deeper parts of the wood. I followed speedily, I hardly knew why	Tearing the girl from my arms, he ran back into the woods, and I followed them

Panel 2
There is still a distance of some yards between them. The man has put his daughter gently on the ground. She is dazed, but sitting, coming around. He has his rifle in his hands and is aiming it at the MONSTER, who is still running towards him.

CAPTION MONSTER V/O	When he saw me draw near, he aimed a gun ...	When he saw me drawing near, he aimed his gun at me ...

Panel 3
The man fires, the bullet (a metal ball in those days) entering and passing through the MONSTER's right shoulder. This knocks him backwards through the air and he cries out in pain.

CAPTION MONSTER V/O	.. and fired!	...and fired!
SFX (from the gun)	KRAKK!	KRAKK!
MONSTER	ARRGH!	ARRGH!
CAPTION MONSTER V/O	I sank to the ground and my injurer escaped into the wood.	I sank to the ground and the man escaped into the wood.

Panel 4
Close up of the MONSTER lying on the ground, his left hand clawing at the air around the wound on his right shoulder. His face is a grimace of agony.

CAPTION MONSTER V/O	I had saved a human being from destruction, and as a recompense I now writhed under the miserable pain of a wound which shattered the flesh and bone! The feelings of kindness gave place to hellish rage. Inflamed by pain, I vowed eternal hatred and vengeance to all mankind!	I'd saved someone's life and as a reward, I had a shattering wound. In great pain, I vowed eternal hatred and vengeance to all mankind.

A page from the script of *Frankenstein* showing the two versions of text.

2. Rough Sketch

The artist first creates a rough sketch from the panel directions provided by the scriptwriter. The artist considers many things at this stage, including story pacing, emphasis of certain elements to tell the story in the best way, and even lighting of the scene.

The rough sketch created from the above script.

As you can see here, Declan is using the central action to provide a lighter background to this page, which is in contrast to the dark borders used elsewhere in the book.

3. Pencils

The artist and Art Director discuss the rough sketches and agree on any changes that are needed. Once a clear direction is established, the artist creates a pencil drawing of the page.

It is interesting to see the changes made from the rough to the pencil. Note how the first two panels have changed drastically, whereas the third and last panel are unchanged. The main panel showing the monster being hit by the gun shot was reversed to allow the direction of the shot from the previous panel to continue.

The pencil drawing of page 76.

4. Inks

From the pencil sketch, an inked version of the same page is created. Inking is not simply tracing over the pencil sketch; it is the process of using black ink to fill in the shaded areas and to add clarity and cohesion to the "pencils". The "inks" give us the final linework prior to the coloring stage.

The inked image, ready for coloring.

5. Coloring

Adding color really brings the page and its characters to life.

There is far more to the coloring stage than simply replacing the white areas with color. Some of the linework is replaced with color (like the red of the shot wound), the light sources are considered for shadows and highlights, and effects added. Finally, the whole page is color-balanced to the other pages of that scene, and to the overall book.

6. Lettering

The final stage is to add the captions, sound effects, and dialogue speech bubbles from the script. These are laid on top of the colored pages. Two versions of each page are lettered, one for each of the two versions of the book (Original Text and Quick Text).

These are then saved as final artwork pages and compiled into the finished book.

Original Text

ISBN:
978-1-906332-49-5

THE CLASSIC NOVEL
BROUGHT TO LIFE IN FULL COLOR!

Quick Text

ISBN:
978-1-906332-50-1

THE FULL STORY IN QUICK MODERN
ENGLISH FOR A FAST-PACED READ!

LOOK OUT FOR MORE TITLES IN THE CLASSICAL COMICS RANGE

Jane Eyre: The Graphic Novel

Published: December 8, 2008 • 144 Pages • $16.95
• Script Adaptation: Amy Corzine • Artwork: John M. Burns • Letters: Terry Wiley

This Charlotte Brontë classic is brought to vibrant life by artist John M. Burns. His sympathetic treatment of Jane Eyre's life in England during the 19th century will delight any reader, with its strong emotions and wonderfully rich atmosphere. Travel back to a time of grand mansions contrasted with the severest poverty, and immerse yourself in this fabulous love story.

A Christmas Carol: The Graphic Novel

Published: November 5, 2008 • 160 Pages • $16.95
• Script Adaptation: Sean Michael Wilson • Pencils: Mike Collins
• Inks: David Roach • Colors: James Offredi • Letters: Terry Wiley

A full-color graphic novel adaptation of the much-loved Christmas story from the great Charles Dickens. Set in Victorian England and highlighting the social injustice of the time, we see one Ebenezer Scrooge go from oppressor to benefactor when he gets a rude awakening to how his life is, and how it should be. With sumptuous artwork and wonderful characters, this magical tale is a must-have for the festive season.

OTHER CLASSICAL COMICS TITLES:

Great Expectations
Published: July 2009
Original Text 978-1-906332-59-4
Quick Text 978-1-906332-60-0

Richard III
Published: September 2009
Original Text 978-1-906332-64-8
Plain Text 978-1-906332-65-5
Quick Text 978-1-906332-66-2

The Tempest
Published: October 2009
Original Text 978-1-906332-69-3
Plain Text 978-1-906332-70-9
Quick Text 978-1-906332-71-6

Romeo & Juliet
Published: November 2009
Original Text 978-1-906332-61-7
Plain Text 978-1-906332-62-4
Quick Text 978-1-906332-63-1

Dracula
Published: February 2010
Original Text 978-1-906332-67-9
Quick Text 978-1-906332-68-6

The Canterville Ghost
Published: March 2010
Original Text 978-1-906332-72-3
Quick Text 978-1-906332-73-0

For more information visit www.classicalcomics.com

TEACHERS' RESOURCES

To accompany each title in our series of graphic novels, we also publish a set of teachers' resources. These widely acclaimed photocopiable books are designed by teachers, for teachers, to help them meet the requirements for the education of ten- to fifteen-year-olds. Each book provides exercises that cover structure, listening, understanding, motivation and comprehension as well as key words, themes and literary techniques. Although the majority of the tasks focus on the use of language in order to align with the revised framework for teaching English, you will also find many cross-curriculum topics, covering areas within history, drama, reading, speaking, writing and art; and with a range of skill levels, they provide many opportunities for differentiated teaching and the tailoring of lessons to meet individual needs.

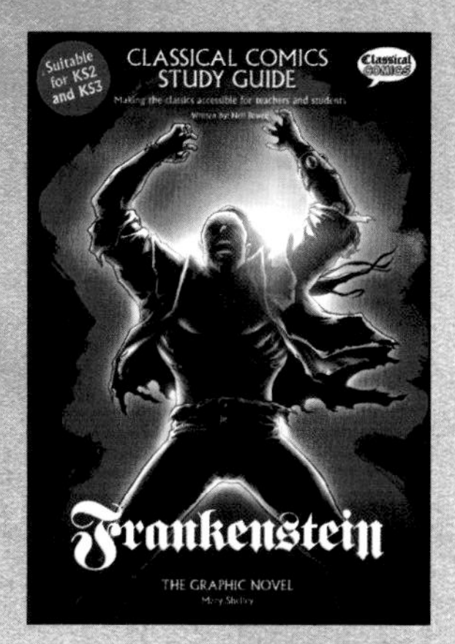

Classical Comics Study Guide: Frankenstein

Black and white, spiral bound A4 (making it easy to photocopy).

Price: $29.99

ISBN: 978-1-906332-56-3

DIFFERENTIATED TEACHING AT YOUR FINGERTIPS!

"Because the exercises feature illustrations from the graphic novel, they provide an immediate link for students between the book and the exercise – however they can also be used in conjunction with any traditional text; and many of the activities can be used completely stand-alone. I think the guide is fantastic and I look forward to using it. I know it will be a great help and lead to engaging lessons . It is easy to use, another major asset. Seriously: well done, well done, well done!"

Kornel Kossuth,
Head of English, Head of General Studies

"Thank you! These will be fantastic for all our students. It is a brilliant resource and to have the lesson ideas too are great. Thanks again to all your team who have created these."

B.P. KS3

"Thank you so much. I can't tell you what a help it will be."

A very grateful teacher, Kerryann SA

"...you've certainly got a corner of East Anglia convinced that this is a fantastic way to teach and progress English literature and language!!" *Chris Mehew*

"With many thanks again for your excellent resources and upbeat philosophy."

Dr. Marcella McCarthy
Leading Teacher for Gifted and Talented Education,
The Cherwell School, Oxford

"Dear Classical Comics,
Can I just say a quick "thank you" for the excellent teachers' resources that accompanied the *Henry V* Classical Comics. I needed to look no further for ideas to stimulate my class. The children responded with such enthusiasm to the different formats for worksheets, it kept their interest and I was able to find appropriate challenges for all abilities. The book itself was read avidly by even the most reluctant readers. Well done, I'm looking forward to seeing the new titles."

A. Dawes, Tockington Manor School

"I wanted to write to thank you - I had a bottom set Y9 class that would have really struggled with the text if it wasn't for your comics, THANK YOU."

Dan Woodhouse

"As to the resource, I can't wait to start using it! Well done on a fantastic service." *Will*

OUR RANGE OF OTHER CLASSICAL COMICS STUDY GUIDES

Henry V	*Macbeth*	*Jane Eyre*	*Frankenstein*	*Great Expectations*
Price: $29.99	Price: $29.99	Price: $29.99	Price: $29.99	Price: $29.99
ISBN: 978-1-906332-53-2	ISBN: 978-1-906332-54-9	ISBN: 978-1-906332-55-6	ISBN: 978-1-906332-56-3	ISBN: 978-1-906332-58-7

BRINGING CLASSICS TO COMIC LIFE

Classical Comics has partnered with Comic Life to bring you a unique comic creation experience!

Comic Life is an award-winning software system that is used and loved by millions of children, adults and schools around the world. The software allows you to create astounding comics in a matter of minutes – and it is really easy and fun to use, too!

Through RM Distribution, you can now obtain all of our titles in every text version, electronically for use with any computer or whiteboard system. In addition, you can also obtain our titles as "No Text" versions that feature just the beautiful artwork without any speech bubbles or captions. These files can then be used in Comic Life (or any other software that can handle jpg files) enabling anyone to create their own version of one of our famous titles.

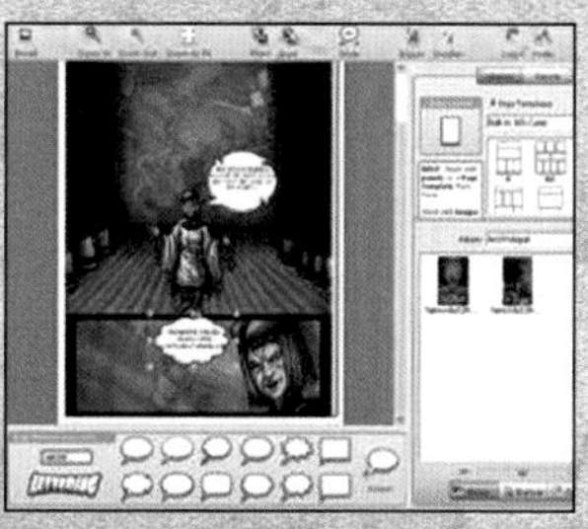

All of the digital versions of our titles are available from RM on a single user or site-license basis. For more details, visit www.rm.com and search for Classical Comics, or visit www.classicalcomics.com/education.

Classical Comics, RM and Comic Life - Bringing Classics to Comic Life!

OUR SHAKESPEARE TITLES ARE AVAILABLE IN THREE TEXT FORMATS

Each text version uses the same exquisite full-color artwork providing a completely flexible reading experience: - you simply choose which version is right for you!

Original Text	THE UNABRIDGED PLAY BROUGHT TO LIFE IN FULL COLOR!
Plain Text	THE COMPLETE PLAY TRANSLATED INTO PLAIN ENGLISH!
Quick Text	THE FULL PLAY IN QUICK MODERN ENGLISH FOR A FAST-PACED READ!

Henry V: The Graphic Novel

Published: November 5, 2008 • 144 Pages • $16.95
• Script Adaptation: John McDonald • Pencils: Neill Cameron • Inks: Bambos • Colors: Jason Cardy & Kat Nicholson • Letters: Nigel Dobbyn

Macbeth: The Graphic Novel

Published: November 5, 2008 • 144 Pages • $16.95
• Script Adaptation: John McDonald • Pencils: & Inks: Jon Haward • Inking Assistant: Gary Erskine • Colors & Letters: Nigel Dobbyn